Acclaim for the Work of ERLE STANLEY GARDNER!

"The best selling author of the century…a master storyteller…A clean, economical writer of peerless ingenuity."
—*New York Times*

"Gardner is humorous, astute, curious, inventive—who can top him? No one has yet."
—*Los Angeles Times*

"A fast and fiery tough tale…very very slick."
—*Kirkus Reviews*

"Erle Stanley Gardner is probably the most widely read of all…authors…His success…undoubtedly lies in the real-life quality of his characters and their problems…"
—*The Atlantic*

"One of the best selling writers of all time, and certainly one of the best selling mystery authors ever."
—*Thrilling Detective*

"Zing, zest and zow are the Gardner hallmark. He will keep you reading at a gallop until The End."
—*Dorothy B. Hughes,*
Mystery Writers of America Grandmaster

I heard running steps on the sidewalk behind the car. It was a woman running. I turned to take a look, and saw Ruth Marr. She was carrying something in her right hand, something that glittered, and her face was frozen into a mask of terror.

She flashed me a swift glance from glassy eyes, started to run on past, and then suddenly checked herself.

"Donald!" she said, in a voice that sounded as though her mouth was dry.

"What is it?"

She climbed into the car and sat down beside me.

"What's that in your hand, Ruth?" I asked.

She shook her head, refusing to meet my eyes. I slid my arm around her shoulders. She was trembling like a dead leaf in a breeze.

"Ruth," I said, "what is it?" and slid my hand down her arm, pulling her hand out into view. Then I switched on the dashlight, took a good look, and switched it back off.

"Thirty-eight caliber, Smith and Wesson police positive," I said. "What's the idea? Did you stage a holdup or something?"

She made a quick, convulsive half turn, flung her arms around my neck, and started to cry...

The Knife
SLIPPED

by Erle Stanley Gardner

WRITING UNDER THE NAME 'A. A. FAIR'

A HARD CASE | HARD CASE CRIME | CRIME NOVEL

A HARD CASE CRIME BOOK
(HCC-127)
First Hard Case Crime edition: December 2016

Published by

Titan Books
A division of Titan Publishing Group Ltd
144 Southwark Street
London SE1 0UP

in collaboration with Winterfall LLC

Print edition ISBN 978-1-78329-927-0
E-book ISBN 978-1-78329-942-3

Design direction by Max Phillips
www.maxphillips.net

Typeset by Swordsmith Productions

The name "Hard Case Crime" and the Hard Case Crime logo
are trademarks of Winterfall LLC. Hard Case Crime books
are selected and edited by Charles Ardai.

Printed in the United States of America

Visit us on the web at www.HardCaseCrime.com

THE KNIFE SLIPPED

Chapter I.

Bertha Cool's secretary was pounding away when I reported at the office, to see whether I worked that day, or sat twiddling my thumbs and speculating whether my monthly wages would total up to anything above Bertha Cool's guarantee.

That guarantee gave me just enough for bare necessities. Working regularly, I could have made a little surplus. So far, I'd never had a full month's work, but, on the other hand, business had never been so slack Bertha Cool had been called on to pay anything under her guarantee.

She was a wise baby, was Bertha Cool. If you made anything out of her, you sure as hell earned it.

The secretary was a good-looking girl—or would have been if she'd given herself a chance. Some discouraging experience in her background had made her feel that she couldn't be bothered with sex appeal, and so she slicked her hair back, used no make-up, and hated men. She didn't seem to get much fun out of life and habitually kept her lips clamped in a tight line as though afraid a word might inadvertently spill out when it wasn't absolutely necessary. For the most part, she made conversation by nodding or shaking her head. If I'd taken the time to have made a form chart, I have an idea the shakes would have outnumbered the nods about three to one.

I closed the door behind me. Its frosted glass bore the legend, "B. COOL, INVESTIGATIONS." A glance at the open door of the private office showed me that Bertha Cool wasn't in. The secretary kept pounding away at her typewriter. I walked over to a chair in the corner, picked up a newspaper, and sat down. I didn't say, "Good morning," or she to me. After you've worked for Bertha Cool just so long, you don't waste social amenities on anyone. I hadn't been working quite that long, but the secretary had.

I read down the front sheet of the newspaper. Half of it was devoted to statements by politicians that the citizens would never have to fight another war on European soil, and listing new legislation that was planned to keep America isolated from European troubles. The other half was devoted to the speeches of high officials calling European rulers liars, crooks, thieves, and gangsters.

I turned over to the sporting section, and wondered if I could find something that looked good enough to carry two dollars of my money on its nose, and if I lost, what I could do without that would save two dollars.

It wasn't an easy problem. When you're working for Bertha Cool, there aren't a lot of economies you can make. She makes them for you.

Over at the typewriter, I heard the sound of banging keys come to a halt as Elsie Brand ripped a letter out of the typewriter and fitted it under the flap of the envelope. She whipped another letterhead from the paper drawer, and looked squarely at me.

"You work today," she said.

I couldn't believe my ears—Elsie Brand actually getting friendly. "No kidding?" I asked. It was a useless question. Elsie Brand wouldn't waste time kidding anybody.

She fed the letterhead with its carbon copy into the roller of the typewriter and ignored the question.

"What kind of a case?" I asked.

"Divorce," she said. "A Mrs.—" She consulted a memo on the desk. "Mrs. Atterby and a Mrs. Cunner."

"What time will Bertha be in?"

"Any minute now."

"What makes you think it's a divorce?" I asked.

"Two women," she said, "both Mrs."

I raised my eyebrows.

"You'll learn," she said, and her fingertips descended on the keyboard of the machine, exploding it into racket.

I turned back to the sporting page with more interest. If I worked today and tomorrow and maybe the next day, I could afford to take a chance on Silver Lining. If, on the other hand, it was only a one-day job—

A big shadow blotted out all the light on the frosted glass panel of the outer door. The knob rattled, and Bertha Cool's avoirdupois came flooding into the room.

Bertha didn't waddle when she walked. She didn't stride. She was big, and she jiggled, but she was hard as nails, physically and mentally. She flowed across that office with the rippling, effortless progress of a cylinder of jelly sliding off a tilted plate.

"Come in, Donald," she said.

I followed her into the private office.

"Shut the door."

I shut it.

"Sit down."

I sat down.

Bertha wasted no time in preliminaries. She was a great believer in not wasting anything which could be turned into money. And as for money itself, she hung onto it like a barnacle caressing the side of a battleship. "We have a divorce case today," she said.

"How long will it last?" I asked.

"I don't know anything about it, just the names. A Mrs. Atterby telephoned Elsie Brand, and asked for a ten o'clock appointment for herself and a Mrs. Cunner."

"Why," I asked, "do two women mean a divorce case?"

She beamed at me. "Jesus, Donald, but you're dumb! About the business, I mean. Don't take offense, my love."

I said nothing.

Bertha Cool lit a cigarette. The quivering flesh around her breasts soaked in the tobacco smoke as she took a deep drag. Her breasts were firm, although her whole chest was enormous. She was big—big all over, and she was completely unrestrained. As she herself expressed it on occasion, "I like loose clothes, loose company, and loose talk, and to hell with the people who don't."

Despite all her size, there was nothing wheezy about her. She stood erect as a granite column, her shoulders flung back, her triple chins hoisted up in the air, her big breasts pushed out in front with perfectly centered "buttons" showing unashamedly through the somewhat flimsy material with which she covered her body on hot days.

She exhaled the tobacco smoke through large nostrils which gave the impression of having been darkened on the inside. "Oh well," she said with a sigh, "someone has to tell you the facts of life, if you're going to be worth a damn in this business. I may as well be the one."

She took another drag at the cigarette, then said, "Most agencies won't touch two types of business. One's divorce business. The other's political investigation. They simply won't handle 'em at any price—the divorce business because it's nasty, the political business because they don't dare.

"All right, that's where we come in, Donald, darling. We'll handle any damn thing on the face of God's green earth that pays money. I haven't got the organization to compete with the big shots, and I have to charge just as large fees, sometimes larger. Therefore I figure that when people come to me, it's a case that other agencies won't touch. So much for that.

"Now then, two married women calling on a detective agency means divorce business because nine times out of ten one's the girl's mother. A married woman thinks her husband is stepping out. She pulls a blonde hair off his coat, and busts into tears. He gives her the best lie he can think up at the moment. She doesn't believe it, but she wants to believe it. Her brain tells her to throw it back in his face. Her heart tells her to cling to it like a drowning man grasping at a straw—Jesus, Donald, I'm getting poetic or romantic or something—I'll have to watch that. You can't have understanding without empathy, and you can't have empathy without losing money. To hell with that stuff. I'm objective, Donald. I have no more feeling than the bullet that leaves a rifle barrel. If it's a charging elephant that's in front of it, the bullet smears him. If it's a poor little deer, nursing a fawn, the slug tears through her vitals just the same. I'm like that, Donald. I'm paid to deliver results, my love, and by God, I deliver 'em."

I nodded. There was no argument on that point. She did.

"Well," she said, "Mama comes for a visit. She holds the daughter's face up to the light, and says, 'Sweetheart, you're not happy. What has that big brute been doing to you?' And then the daughter starts to cry, and pretty quick she tells Mama her suspicions, and Mama takes the girl by the hand and—"

Elsie Brand opened the door, and said, "Mrs. Atterby and Mrs. Cunner."

Bertha Cool beamed all over her face. "Show them in," she said, "show them in."

Elsie Brand backed away from the door. She didn't need to say anything. The woman who came striding past her wasn't one to wait for invitation. She was a hatchet-faced battle-ax with high cheekbones, big, black eyes with dark pouches underneath, a mouth which was a straight gash across her face, a nose like the prow of a battleship, and a long, determined stride which indicated her feet knew damn well she was going someplace to make trouble, and wanted to get her there as soon as possible.

Her face was the color of a tropical sunset with rouge over the cheeks, and crimson lipstick trying to turn the upper lip into a cupid's bow. The thing must have been weird enough so far as the average spectator is concerned, but to a detective who trains himself to look closely and see plenty of details, it looked like an oil painting done by Aunt Kate or Cousin Edith, the kind that are hung in a dark corner in the dining room where the open kitchen door will hide 'em during mealtimes.

Behind her, came a red-eyed woman about twenty-five years younger, inclined to fat—not the hard, determined fat of Bertha Cool, but the sagging fat which pulls the muscles down until the body starts looking like a melting snowman.

Bertha Cool got up and beamed across the desk. "Mrs. Atterby?" she asked of the battle-ax.

Mrs. Atterby nodded, and looked at Bertha Cool with disappointed eyes.

Bertha Cool turned to the pink-eyed one, and said, "You're Mrs. Cunner. Do be seated. —This is Donald Lam, one of my operatives."

Mrs. Atterby didn't sit down. She swung around to face me. I saw her chin go up in the air another notch. I listened, waiting to hear her sniff. She didn't sniff, but she might as well have done so. Her reaction was obvious.

Mrs. Cunner sat down—apparently, always glad to take her weight off her feet.

Bertha Cool said to Mrs. Atterby, "Sit down, dearie. Don't run your blood pressure up, thinking that because I'm a woman, and Donald is a little runt, we can't handle your work, because we can. I'm tougher than shoe leather, and Donald here is just plain poison.

"You'll like him when you know him better. He started out to be a lawyer. They disbarred him because he told a client how to commit a murder and get away with it. The bar association said Donald was all wet, of course, but his ethics were bad. —And do you know, the little bastard was right all the time. After they disbarred him, he actually pulled it, and made it stand up. He has brains, that boy."

Mrs. Atterby said, "Since you've brought the subject up yourself, Mrs. Cool—or is it *Miss* Cool—?"

"Mrs.," Bertha Cool said, "and don't pull your punches, dearie, because, after all, you haven't a leg to stand on. The big detective agencies won't touch your kind of case with a ten-foot pole, and you know it, or you wouldn't be here. If we don't handle your case, no one will. So sit down and tell us your troubles, and don't mind if I cuss because I'm profane as hell when I get started."

There was a sudden glint in Mrs. Atterby's eyes. It was almost as though she recognized a kindred spirit. She sat down.

"Smoke?" Bertha Cool asked.

Mrs. Atterby shook her head. I figured painting that mouth on took too much time and effort to risk taking any chances with it.

Mrs. Cool shifted her eyes to Mrs. Cunner.

Mrs. Atterby answered the unspoken question for her. "No," she said, "she's not smoking. She's too upset."

As though the words were her cue, the younger woman fished a soggy handkerchief from her purse, shoved it halfway up to her eyes, then held it there, bravely fighting back tears.

"Well," Bertha Cool said cheerfully, "let's start the ball rolling. Time is money, you know."

Mrs. Atterby looked at Mrs. Cunner. "Tell her, Edith," she said.

Edith immediately made a nose dive for the depths of the soggy handkerchief.

Bertha Cool regarded her with steady, calm, almost disinterested appraisal, then shifted her eyes to Mrs. Atterby.

Mrs. Atterby said, "The poor child is *so* upset. She's never had anything like this. She's always been sheltered from the sordid facts of life. I didn't keep her in the darkness of ignorance; but I will say there was never a girl with a cleaner, sweeter, purer mind than Edith Atterby, and all of our friends realized it. I don't know what it was that attracted her to Eben, unless it was the very contrast. Eben is a worldly man, and I knew the minute I set eyes on him that he wasn't half good enough for Edith, but she *would* insist on going around with him. I told her— Well, I won't go into that now, but Edith herself will be the first to admit that if she'd taken her mother's advice years ago, this would never have happened."

Edith pulled out the louder stop, and the sobs became distinctly audible.

"All right," Bertha Cool said cheerfully, "tell us about it, and let's get started."

Mrs. Atterby glanced at me. "I don't want to embarrass Edith," she said, "if there were no man here, just us women, and—"

"Oh nuts," Bertha Cool interrupted. "How long's she been married?"

"Five years."

Bertha Cool said, "Let's quit beating around the bush. What's her husband doing, cheating around, going to whorehouses, or keeping a mistress?"

Edith Cunner raised startled, tear-reddened eyes to stare at Mrs. Cool.

Mrs. Atterby said reproachfully, in a low voice, "I always use the word 'houses of prostitution' in talking to Edith, Mrs. Cool."

"I don't. I call 'em whorehouses," Bertha said acidly. "It's easier to say. It's more expressive, and it leaves no room for doubt."

"Well," Mrs. Atterby sniffed, "at least Eben hasn't sunk that low—although I don't know but what it would be preferable to what he has done. After all, association with prostitutes indicates a man is merely giving vent to his coarse animal nature. It isn't as direct and studied an insult to a wife as what Eben is doing."

"Who is she?" Bertha Cool asked.

"Who?"

"The mistress."

Mrs. Atterby said to Edith, "Tell her about *that woman*, Edith, dear."

Edith said, chokingly, "She—He's k-k-keeping her in an ap-ap-apartment."

"Who is she?" Bertha Cool asked.

"We don't know," Mrs. Atterby said. "That's why we came here."

"Oh," Bertha Cool observed.

"We want to find out."

"What do you know about her?"

Mrs. Atterby launched into voluble speech. "When Edith and Eben were first married," she said, "Eben seemed a most devoted husband. There was a time when I almost thought that I'd wronged the man. Of course, Edith was far too good for him, and I think she came to realize that only a short time after the marriage. But Edith is intensely loyal, and she wouldn't admit it even to her own mother."

She turned to Edith, and said, "You remember, Edith, how many, many times I asked you, and you always insisted that you were absolutely happy."

"I w-w-was," Edith sobbed.

Bertha Cool said, "Oh for Christ's sake, cut out the weeps! By God, you'd think your husband was the only man on earth who ever stepped out. They all do—those that are able. Personally, I wouldn't have a man who was true to me, not that I'd want him to flaunt his affairs in my face or to the neighborhood, but a man who doesn't step out once in a while isn't worth the powder and shot to blow him to hell."

Mrs. Atterby raised her brows. "Have *you* ever had a daughter who was married?" she asked with dignity.

"No," Bertha Cool said, "I've had a husband."

Mrs. Atterby said, "Well, we can leave the ethics of the situation out of the discussion. I think I have told you that Edith is a little different from most women. Edith, even if I do say it myself, is of finer clay. She—"

"Twenty-five dollars a day," Bertha Cool interrupted. "That covers eight hours investigation and office supervision. We make written reports. If you want three operatives on the job, it'll cost you forty dollars a day. That'll give you a twenty-four hour service—personally, I don't recommend it. If a man's stepping out at all, one operative, picking him up at five o'clock in the evening when he leaves the office and working until one o'clock in the morning, can get all the dirt. When a man's promoting something new, he works late hours trying to make the grade.

After he's made the sale, he has a dinner, a little petting and is on his way home by ten o'clock. Married men get so they make a routine even of keeping a mistress. I tried two of 'em—and never gave a damn for either one. They're lousy lovers."

Mrs. Atterby said, "Mrs. Cool! Please! Edith's only a child, you know."

Bertha Cool blew out cigarette smoke. "Twenty-five dollars a day," she said.

"Twenty-five dollars a day is a lot of money," Mrs. Atterby snapped.

"Seems like it is to you," Bertha Cool said easily, "not to me."

Mrs. Atterby hesitated. Her long, lean fingers gripped the black, patent-leather handbag which was supported on her lap. "You guarantee results?" she asked.

"Hell no," Bertha Cool said, "we don't guarantee anything. Christ, what do you want us to do, *get* him seduced? My God, the man *may* be true to her. I can put a shadow on him and we can find out. —That's what you want, ain't it, dearie?"

"In a way, yes. In another way, we feel there's no question of his guilt. You should agree to furnish absolute proof of it at that figure."

Bertha Cool said, "No dice, dearie. Either fish or cut bait. I'm busy."

"You're in a position to start immediately?"

"Yes."

"And we can discontinue the service at any time?"

"At any time," Bertha Cool said. "Only fractions of a day don't count. Hell, I'm not going to get up at eleven o'clock at night to tell an operative the job's been discontinued so you can get a rebate on one-fourth of a day."

"We wouldn't expect you to," Mrs. Atterby said, magnanimously.

"I thought you might," Bertha Cool observed.

"Well," Mrs. Atterby said, "if those are your *best* terms—?"

"Best, final, and only," Bertha Cool said, and in her voice each word was as final as the driving home of a nail.

"Well, we could hire you for one night and see what—"

"Hundred dollar minimum," Bertha Cool interrupted.

"You mean that if you get the evidence in one night, you would still expect us to pay for three more?"

Bertha Cool blew out more smoke. "That's right, dearie."

"That seems—"

"Take it or leave it," Bertha Cool said.

The women exchanged glances. "When," Mrs. Atterby asked, "would that be payable?"

Bertha Cool met her eyes. "Now."

Mrs. Atterby sighed defeat. She opened her purse, and took out four twenties. She said to Edith, "Let mother have that twenty she gave you this morning, darling."

Edith dabbed the handkerchief to her eyes, opened her purse, and handed twenty dollars across to Mrs. Atterby. Mrs. Atterby put the five twenty-dollar bills on Bertha Cool's desk. Bertha Cool signed her name to a printed receipt, filled in Mrs. Atterby's name and the figure of one hundred dollars, and handed the receipt across to Mrs. Atterby. She pulled spectacles from her bag, adjusted them to her hawk-like nose, and read through every word of the fine print, not bothering to conceal her suspicions.

"It says here that if we order the investigation discontinued for any reason whatever, you are to keep all of the money which has heretofore been paid, that at the expiration of four days, we pay twenty-five dollars additional for each day we desire your service."

"That's right," Bertha Cool said.

"But suppose we should find that you were—that you were incompetent to handle the matter?"

Bertha Cool said, "I'm not incompetent, dearie. I put that clause in there because I'm hard-boiled. Usually I hurt the clients' feelings. I don't have time to kid them along. Occasionally I cuss like hell. I've talked with you more than I usually talk with a client without getting cash."

"Your reports will be complete?" Mrs. Atterby asked.

"Leave it to Donald," Bertha Cool said.

I could feel Mrs. Atterby shift her eyes in my direction and study my face, but I didn't turn around to meet her eyes.

Mrs. Atterby pocketed the receipt. Bertha Cool got down to business. She said to Edith, "Take that handkerchief away from your face, dearie, and talk clearly and distinctly. Where do you live?"

"Sixty-two nineteen Hawthorne Avenue."

"How old are you?"

"Twenty-nine."

"Where does your husband work?"

"He's an assistant lawyer at the—the—"

"Don't do it," Bertha Cool said, without emotion, as Edith Cunner showed symptoms of more tears. "Bawl later if you want. Give me the dope now. What's the name of that place where your hubby works?"

"The Webley McMarr Wholesale Company."

"What makes you think he's been cheating on you?"

"He—he's been away from home nights. He says he's been working, but—but a neighbor saw him—saw him in a night-club—"

Mrs. Atterby took up the narrative. "Saw him in a night-club," she said, "in evening clothes, entertaining a dizzy blonde who wasn't wearing a stitch more than the law allowed. You can see what that means, Mrs. Cool. He has some place to change his clothes. His tuxedo was at home in the closet all the time. Edith is certain he hadn't taken it out. Yet, there he was, in this nightclub, entertaining this blonde, and wearing *evening* clothes. That must mean that he has an apartment where he's keeping another set of clothes and—"

"And the blonde?" Bertha Cool finished.

"Exactly."

"Any other evidence?" Bertha Cool asked.

"Good heavens, isn't that enough?"

Bertha Cool's big shoulders heaved in a shrug. She shifted her eyes back to Edith Cunner. "D'ju ask him about it, Edith?"

Edith shook her head, and said, "Mother thought best not to."

"I certainly did," Mrs. Atterby said. "I saw no reason for letting him tell the poor child a lot of lies. He's lied to her before. She doesn't realize it, but I did, just as soon as she told me some of the things he'd told her. I *knew* they were lies. Edith doesn't know the world. Thank heavens, the child was spared some of the things I've been through."

"What do you want *us* to do?" Bertha Cool asked.

"Find the apartment," Mrs. Atterby said, "catch them red-handed, have her arrested and taken to the police station, the shameless little strumpet."

"Perhaps she doesn't know he's married."

"It makes no difference. She's living with him in sin. If you ask me, this younger generation is altogether too careless about their morals. If they were taken to jail occasionally, they'd make it a point to find out with whom they were associating. And when a girl goes to an apartment with a man—to say nothing of living there with him—" Mrs. Atterby sniffed.

Bertha Cool said, to Edith Cunner, "What's he look like?"

"He's tall, almost six feet, very straight and thin. He has reddish hair—sort of a chestnut. It waves back from his forehead, and his profile—well, his chin—"

"His chin goes back in under his upper teeth," Mrs. Atterby said. "Edith can't say that I didn't warn her about a man with a weak chin. She—"

Bertha Cool, having got the hundred dollars, wasn't wasting any more time. "All right," she said, "we can recognize him. We'll pick him up at the office. Does he leave at five or five-thirty?"

"Five," Edith Cunner said.

"Is he coming home tonight?"

"As far as I know," she said.

"All right, we'll pick him up. Don't say anything about your suspicions. Above all, don't get soft and start weeping on his shoulder, let him tell you he was entertaining an out-of-town customer, and then confess that you've employed a detective to shadow him. That *always* results in the detective getting beaten up, and Donald can't stand too many beatings. He's so frail I have to take care of him. He ain't a man who can stand a beating and be on the job ready to go to work the next morning. It makes him sick all over when he gets beaten up. So, having gone this far, you act as though nothing had happened, and give us a chance. Do you understand?"

Edith nodded.

"That means dry your eyes, quit thinking about it, and be happy," Mrs. Cool said. "Lots of times a man will lay off the rough stuff if he thinks his wife is sick, or nervous. Lots of times he thinks she's found out when she's pulling a lot of weeps, and gets afraid to take chances for a while. You want to build up his confidence, make him think he's getting away with it, and everything is fine. In that way, we can get the evidence quicker."

"As I understand this receipt," Mrs. Atterby said, "it doesn't make any difference to us whether you get the evidence tonight or three nights from now."

"It does to us," Bertha Cool said. "Have you got a lawyer?"

"Not yet."

"Going to ask for a divorce?"

"Of course she is," Mrs. Atterby said, as Edith hesitated.

"Any property?" Mrs. Cool wanted to know.

"He has a good salary."

"Any children?"

"No, thank heavens," Mrs. Atterby interpolated, "at least the girl has been spared the humiliation of having children who would learn of their father's escapades."

Bertha Cool looked appraisingly at Edith Cunner. "How much do you weigh?" she asked.

Edith's face showed surprise. "A hundred and fifty-three," she said.

"Stripped?" Bertha Cool inquired.

"Stripped."

"How long have you been married?"

"Five years."

"What did you weigh when you got married?"

"A hundred and fourteen."

Bertha Cool's silence was eloquent.

"Edith *should* watch her figure," Mrs. Atterby said, "but then—" She broke off, and looked significantly at Bertha Cool.

"I know," Bertha Cool said. "I'm fat. I could get fat on a diet of nothing but drinking water. When I was a hundred and twenty, I could put on ten pounds in two weeks just by putting a little butter on my toast in the morning. I fought my figure until I found *my* husband was stepping out on *me*. Then I called him on it, told him it was all right for him to have mistresses if he wanted, but if he wanted to revel in blondes, I was damned if I was going to deny myself butter. Of course," Bertha Cool went on, "I did take steps to see the man wasn't blackmailed. I picked out his mistresses for him—although to his dying day, he never suspected it. I put on seventy-five pounds in less than two years. And never felt better in my life—but I'm self-supporting. *I* don't have to marry again."

She looked at Mrs. Atterby and then at the door. Mrs. Atterby got up. "Come, Edith," she said, and then, as an afterthought, turned to Bertha Cool, and said, "Well, you can't really blame Edith. Eben insists that Edith cook the richest foods and lots of them. The poor child doesn't have a chance to watch her figure—not unless she'd go to the trouble of cooking two meals, one for herself, and another one for him. He's frightfully inconsiderate."

Bertha Cool looked at Edith Cunner as a horse buyer would survey a mare. "Better think it over, dearie," she said, "before you dash into the divorce court. If you get rid of one man, you've got to get yourself another. They aren't exactly plentiful, and competition is pretty keen."

"How *can* you look at it in that way?" Mrs. Atterby asked. "To think of the poor dear child living with a man who's carrying on an affair with another woman! Of course she can't! But he'll pay for what he's done. Don't you forget that. He'll pay."

Bertha Cool didn't say anything. She glanced at me. I held the door open until they had left, and then pushed it shut.

Bertha Cool caressed the five twenty-dollar bills with her fat but sturdy fingers. "Jesus Christ, Donald," she said, "they got on my nerves. I wonder if you hate people like that as bad as I do."

"Ten times worse," I told her fervently.

She looked at me then, her gray eyes suddenly turning cold and hard. "Don't forget, Donald, darling, that you have a living to make. It isn't what we *want* to do that puts fat on our bones. It is what we do."

I said meaningfully, "There isn't much fat on *my* bones."

She jiggled all over in appreciation. "You're *so* droll, Donald," she said. "But you know I couldn't possibly give you a raise—not the way business is, Donald, my love. There's a depression on."

I kept quiet.

"Now, don't be sullen, Donald. I hate this just as badly as you do, but the world is a cruel place, after all. Remember, when you were walking the streets looking for work, Donald? And there just isn't work to be had—particularly for a disbarred lawyer who can't get references from his last employer."

She regarded me with twinkling eyes.

"Are you trying to tell me that you wouldn't give me a recommendation?"

"Not if you quit and left me in the lurch, Donald, dear—and not if I had to fire you for refusal to follow orders. Now, don't look at me like that. You'd better get a little sleep if you're going to be on the job tonight. And if you lose him, Donald, don't try to fake your report so it'll look as though you didn't. That's an old trick, Donald, and I know all the old tricks—and some of the new ones. Being new to the game, they might seem like good ideas to you. Of course, we'll fake the reports to the client, lover, but that's different. Between you and me, there must be absolute honesty. Do you understand?"

"I'll need some expense money," I said, "and a car."

"You will that," she told me. "I'll have my car here in front of the place at four-thirty. It'll be filled with gas and oil. You'll need some expense money for incidentals. I suppose you'll need a dinner. You won't have time to eat much, just something you can grab. You can get a very good hamburger sandwich for fifteen cents, and you may have to put in two or three telephone calls—say fifteen cents more. Here's fifty cents, Donald, and remember to keep a detailed expense account."

Chapter II.

Webley & McMarr was a good-sized jobbing outfit dealing in garage and automobile accessories, light tools and machinery, some brands of oils which they put under their own name, a line of tires made for the jobbing trade, and their own brand of sparkplug.

A line of showcases ranged along one side of the building. Sales and executive officers were back of these. A sign announced that buyers' offices were on the upper floor.

I had an old briefcase which I'd filled with newspapers until it bulged and I walked boldly down the long corridor and climbed the stairs. A sign announced that buying hours were from two to four. It was then four-thirty-five, but a couple of salesmen were still seated dejectedly in the waiting room. Off from this room was a glass-enclosed secretarial office with a desk, a telephone, and a switchboard, presided over by a sallow-faced, beak-nosed woman. Back of her desk were two doors. Each door here bore the same legend—simply the words ASSISTANT BUYER.

The woman looked up when I entered the waiting room. I hesitated a moment, then diffidently crossed over to the swinging glass door.

She said, in a harsh, rasping voice, "Whadda yuh want?"

"Mr. Cunner," I said.

"Busy. Buying hours two to four. Who you with?"

I recognized the wisdom of the management in putting a girl like that in charge. Even a traveling salesman would draw the line at her. I figured she knew all the kidding approaches so I shifted my gaze to the carpet, and tried to look as though I was getting ready to bust out crying.

"What is it?" she asked, just a note of sympathy in her voice.

I looked up desperately. "Would you mind asking Mr. Cunner if he got Mr. Beppler's message about Mr. Smith?"

"You're Smith?" she asked.

I nodded.

"Who you with?" she repeated.

I fidgeted again, and said, "If he—would it be too much to ask him if he got that message? I—I can wait until he comes out."

"No, you can't," she said. "That's out. You haven't been with this game very long, have you? Buttonholing a buyer on his way home from work is the quickest way to get in bad. —You wait here. I'll see."

She got up and moved toward the door on the right. I figured about where the desk should be and moved so that I could see through the crack in the door. She pushed it open, and went in. I couldn't see anything.

I shifted my position a couple of steps.

As she opened the door to come out, I saw a tall, good-looking man, around thirty-five with wavy, chestnut hair, straight nose and a receding chin, sitting at a desk signing mail.

She came over to me and said, "He doesn't know any Mr. Beppler, and there was no message about a Mr. Smith. Come back tomorrow at two o'clock, and wait your turn."

"Do you suppose I could—"

"No," she said.

"Just for a minute."

"No."

I thanked her and walked out. The two salesmen waiting in the reception room regarded me patronizingly as I walked past.

I went out and sat in the car, waiting.

Eben Cunner came out in the midst of a whole mess of people at seven minutes past five. He took a B-Street car, and I nursed Bertha Cool's agency automobile into action and limped along behind. The B-Street car didn't go anyways near Hawthorne Avenue. So I figured I'd picked a live lead right from the start.

Webley & McMarr were pretty well on the outskirts of the wholesale district. The B-Street car was going toward the center of the city. As we got closer to the office district, the congestion got worse. Cunner got off at a place where the safety zone was crowded with people waiting for cars. Streams of pedestrians were pouring across the intersections with the signal. I figured I was all washed up before I'd started, but luck was with me. He waited at the corner for the signal to change, crossed the street when I did, and turned into a garage.

I'd had visions of trying to explain to Bertha Cool how I'd made the mistake of following him into the congested district with a car, when I should have been on foot; but now I brightened considerably. Going into the garage meant he'd be coming out with a car. If I'd been on foot, I'd have had to let him go or else get a taxi. Bertha Cool's expense accounts didn't provide for taxicabs—particularly over long distance.

I turned into the garage. An attendant came forward to hand me a parking slip. I told him I only wanted information about a monthly rate. I said I'd landed a job nearby and was trying to figure a good parking place. He looked the car over, and told me I'd better get one in the parking lots. They were cheaper. I turned the heap around, and managed to stall the conversation along until Eben Cunner came flashing out in a car that was so shiny you could use the sides for a shaving mirror.

Cunner's car purred up the incline to the street, and Bertha Cool's transportation system rattled along behind.

Through the traffic, I didn't have much trouble. He had lots of pickup and better brakes, but a longer wheel base, and he was afraid of getting his fenders scratched. There was nothing to worry about on the fenders of the car Bertha Cool had dug up for her operatives to drive.

We fought our way through the snarl of five-thirty traffic, and Cunner turned into one of the through boulevards for north-bound traffic. I gave Bertha's jalopy everything it had, trying to keep up.

Cunner was a good driver. He sat back of the wheel, smoking a cigarette, and whisked his bus through openings in the traffic. It was a swell car, just a whisper of acceleration from the motor and it would shoot through an opening that would close up before I could get my car coaxed into moving any faster.

Along at thirty-five miles an hour, my heap covered the ground, but when I stepped on the gas for a quick getaway, all of the excess power went into piston-slaps, bearing-knocks, and noises of protest from under the hood. After four or five seconds of noisy remonstrance, the motor would pick up sluggish speed. I tagged along as best I could. A couple of breaks on traffic signals gave me a chance to catch up. Then he got the breaks. When he was just about far enough ahead to make me figure I was through, he swung into the curb and parked.

It was a good thing I was fairly far behind him. It took quite a bit of manipulating, and an argument with a truck driver, to get into the curb fifty feet behind him. It wasn't a place where there was much parking, and I figured I looked too conspic-uous. I was thinking about going on past him and waiting for him to catch up, when one of the yellow streetcars came swaying along the boulevard, holding up a whole swarm of impatient traffic behind it. The motorman was contributing to the industrial noise of a great city by larruping hell out of the bell every time an automobile would sneak through and turn onto the track ahead of him.

The streetcar grated to a stop, and I could hear the sound of automobile tires on the pavement for a block and a half back.

A lone passenger got off the streetcar. She waved a gloved hand to Cunner, and held up traffic while she crossed over to the sidewalk.

I glanced at my three-dollar wristwatch, jerked out a notebook, and made a hasty scrawl. "Five-thirty-two, party joined by snappy blonde about twenty-four or twenty-five who leaves 'M' car at second boulevard stop behind bridge on North Sinclair Boulevard."

I didn't have time to put the book and pencil away, but tossed them to the seat, and eased the agency wreck into motion as Cunner glided out into traffic. The streetcar, with its collection of motorlights behind it, had groaned on ahead, so I was in a space reasonably free from cars. Now that Cunner shipped the blonde, he loafed along at a conservative thirty to thirty-five miles an hour, and didn't fight traffic. I fought my way up behind him.

Cars had commenced to show headlights, and that made it easier to keep my tailing job from being too conspicuous. I'd memorized the license number of Cunner's automobile when he drove it out of the garage, and when we ran into a closed signal, just at the change, I had a chance to jot it down—also the name of the garage where he was storing it.

Out to the north of town, to the left of where the through boulevards merge into the state highway, there's a real-estate venture called Yucca City. Two years ago it was steep hills. Now it's "exclusive hillside terraces." A sign said so. What level ground there was had been given over to a little business district. When Cunner turned his car to the left and purred up the hill toward Yucca City, I gave Bertha Cool's mechanical abortion all of the gas it would take, and settled back against the seat awaiting developments. For a while I figured the main bearing was going to give way and let the crankshaft fly out and wrap itself around my neck. But the old bus held together until we reached the top of the grade. Steam was hissing out of the overflow pipe, and hot water had splashed out around the leaky gasket in the radiator cap to stain the hood and windshield. But we'd made it. Cunner drove to the Yucca Club, a swanky place which blossomed out with a floorshow later and had a glassed-in dancing platform, built out over a sidehill from which could be seen the lights of the metropolitan district clustered like stars.

Cunner and the blonde parked in front of the cocktail lounge. A uniformed attendant took charge of the car. I had a chance to get a look at the blonde as she got out of the car. While the attendant was driving it away, I crossed out the twenty-five in my notebook for the blonde's age, and made it twenty-seven. I also added "Beautiful legs" to the description. I wasn't so certain Bertha Cool would appreciate the detail, but I knew damn well the mother-in-law would.

I found a place down the street to park my bus, and gave the motor a chance to recuperate. I went back and glanced in the cocktail bar, then looked around for a telephone. I couldn't find any except in the back of the cocktail bar, and decided to chance it. I walked on past the stools where Cunner and the girl were talking in low voices while the bartender was shaking up a couple of cocktails. I couldn't hear what was being said, but the blonde was doing the talking. Her voice was the kind that made ripples run up and down a man's backbone. It was one of those seductive voices that came as a cooing caress to the masculine eardrum. She was as conscious of her sex as a kid is of a new bicycle on Christmas morning.

I went back to the telephone booth, called Bertha Cool's agency, and got my dime back. Then I called her apartment, and got her on the line.

"Oh yes, Donald," she said, when I told her I had a report. "Wait a minute, my love," she added, "I'm half undressed over a Scotch and soda. I'll have to get a pencil."

It took her a couple of minutes. When she came back to the line, I gave her the license number of the automobile, the name of the garage, and reported progress.

"Stay right with 'em, Donald," she said. "Don't let them out of your sight."

"I'll do the best I can," I told her. "That bus of his starts from scratch and gets up to fifty miles an hour before it's reached the next intersection."

I got no sympathy from Bertha Cool. "My operatives are supposed to be good drivers," she said, and hung up.

I stuck around the telephone booth for a while, watching them, trying to decide whether the girl was really gone on him, or playing him for a good thing. Offhand, it wouldn't look as though the assistant buyer for a wholesale store could be much of a Santa Claus, but I had the evidence of that brand-new car to think about.

After a while, I left the phone booth and went out. The blonde was still talking. She'd drained her cocktail all at once. Cunner's was about half empty. The bartender was shaking up two more.

It was pretty dark by the time I got outside and settled in my car. I was hungry, but I didn't dare to leave them on the strength of that second cocktail—not at the rate the blonde was wrapping herself around hers. I figured that when they came out with those two cocktails under their belts, they'd make that car do its stuff, and I looked over my heap with a skeptical eye. However, I'd do my best. If they stayed out in the ten-cent phone call district, I only had enough money to make one more report to Bertha Cool. I figured I'd save that until around ten o'clock—if I could keep them in sight that long.

After about twenty minutes, when they hadn't come out, I walked over to the cocktail lounge. They weren't there. I went back to use the phone, called information, and asked for the number of the B. Cool Detective Agency. Information gave me my coin back—also the wrong number. The bartender didn't seem particularly suspicious. A few other customers had drifted in, and he was reasonably lazy. I rubbered into the main dining room. Cunner and his girlfriend were being served soup. I figured that meant dinner, and went out to find myself something to eat.

There wasn't any place in the neighborhood, and I was hungry. I coaxed my crate into motion and rattled down the main drag to a sandwich place. I got a sandwich for fifteen cents. It was lousy. Bertha Cool was supposed to furnish expenses when I was working on a job. She paid for the sandwich. I had to tap my own resources for the muddy coffee that went with it, but I was saving on what I'd have had to pay at the greasy spoon where I ate when I wasn't working nights, so I tossed a nickel into the kitty and figured I was ahead at that. I stuck around for a cigarette and bummed a copy of the racing edition off the proprietor. Silver Lining with my two dollars on his nose had romped in two lengths ahead of the field. The bet paid eight to one, so I felt like a picture star on the loose. I blew myself to one mince pie a la mode, and rattled back to the Yucca Club.

It was pretty early for action there, but there were a few customers in the main dining room. The place catered to an early
supper trade, and then tried to pick up whoopee couples with
floorshows later in the evening. The orchestra was grinding out
a waltz, and lights had been turned down in the glass-enclosed
dining room. Lights from the city below were grouped in twinkling clusters. Cunner and the blonde were dancing. The way
she danced was something her grandparents hadn't ever dreamt
about, or they'd have called the deal off before she got here. I
went back and sat in the car.

After half an hour, clouds drifted in from the west, and
blotted out the stars. Mist began to settle over the foothills. It
got pretty cold. I could still see the lights of town. Over in the
Yucca Club, lights would blaze on for a while, then die down to
a blue moonlit effect. The dance orchestra sounded joyful and
jazzy.

I kept waiting and shivering.

At seven-forty-eight, Cunner and the blonde came out. The
parking attendant delivered their car, and I started my motor.

I tailed their taillights along a fairly level road, passed the
"business" district of Yucca City, and saw them drive into the
garage of a big white apartment house built on a spur of the hill
with a commanding view. A red neon sign blazing the words
"MOUNTAIN CREST APARTMENTS" was surrounded with a
blood-red aura where the particles of moisture from the clouds
had slid down the mountainside in the last half hour.

I stuck around and waited. After a while, I got out and went
into the garage on a rubberneck expedition.

A couple of one-dollar bills and a hot tip on a racehorse would
have done wonders, but Bertha Cool didn't do business that
way. I had to rely on cheek and gab. The man in charge of the
garage did janitor work in the apartment house during the day.

He was a Swede, and inclined to be surly, but he had one of my cigarettes and listened to my story. I was a chauffeur out of work and without a lead. I was looking over the swankier apartments, figuring on a prospect. I'd be willing to work for damn near nothing. I looked over the cars, asked questions about a couple of the better-looking crates, and picked Cunner's car on my third bet.

The janitor wasn't particularly communicative. I learned that the car belonged to a Mr. A. L. Gell, a man who had something to do with the racetrack. He was a bachelor—divorced. His sister was a "nice woman" who sometimes came through with a hot tip on the ponies.

When the Swede dried up, I went back and got in my car.

After a while, I heard the staccato roar of motorcycles, and a couple of speed cops drove up. They parked their machines, kicked the foot supports into place, and went into the apartment house. They were gone about twenty minutes. A while later they came back out, and went away. A police machine drove up. I spotted it by the license plate. The man who was driving it wasn't in uniform. He went on into the apartment house, and came back after a while. Then along toward eleven o'clock, a couple of boys from the fire department dropped in.

I left my car and barged on in after the two guys from the fire department. There was a girl with chestnut hair and big brown eyes at a switchboard. A night clerk was on duty, puttering around with books. It didn't give me much of a jolt when I heard the guys from the fire department ask for Mr. Gell. The girl at the switchboard said, "What name please?" And one of the men said awkwardly, "Just tell him that Premmer sent us."

The girl plugged in a line, said something I couldn't hear

into the mouthpiece, then turned to the men, and said, "Go on up. He's expecting you. Apartment six hundred."

I went out and took dope on the automobile, and kicked myself for not having done the same trick with the speed cops and the police car. It was a hell of a way to run a love nest. If I'd have been up there with that blonde, I certainly wouldn't have invited the Los Angeles officers to drop in for the evening.

I figured it might be just as well not to attract the attention of the telephone operator right then. There were a couple of glass-doored telephone booths across from her desk. One of them with the figure "1" over the door was a pay-station telephone which didn't go through the switchboard. The other was numbered "2," and had a desk telephone which was connected with the house. I ducked into booth "1," took down the receiver, and dropped a dime. I gave the operator the number of Bertha Cool's apartment. After a while, I heard her voice coming over the line, cool and competent. "All right, Donald, my love, what is it now?"

"Just a report," I said.

"Report of what, lover?"

"Progress."

"How much progress?"

"I don't know. I've tailed Cunner and this blonde girl to an apartment just outside the business district of Yucca City. It's rather a fancy joint called the Mountain Crest Apartments. He has an apartment under the name of A. L. Gell."

"The blonde?" Bertha Cool asked with businesslike efficiency.

"She's his sister," I said.

"Oh yeah?" Bertha Cool asked.

"Uh huh, and they have visitors."

"What sort of visitors, Donald?"

"Funny visitors. Visitors who drive official cars, two speed cops, a police officer in a prowl car, and right now two firemen—all driving city cars."

"Official business, Donald?"

"I wouldn't know," I told her.

Bertha Cool's voice showed a sudden increase in interest. "Where are you now, Donald?"

"Talking from a telephone booth in the Mountain Crest Apartments—right close to the elevators, and the two firemen are up there now. I tailed them in and heard them tell the girl at the switchboard Premmer had sent them."

"Any initials, Donald?"

"No initials, just Premmer, and here are the license numbers on the automobile."

I read the license numbers off to her, and she said, "There may be more to this than just a divorce job, Donald. Don't let him get away from you."

I laughed at that crack and said, "Listen, it's just luck I've stayed with him as long as I have. The heap you gave me will cover the ground, but that's all you can say for it. Any time he quits being interested in that blonde and concentrates on the road ahead, I'll be left so far behind I can't even smell the exhaust fumes."

She said, "Do the best you can, Donald, and remember if he gives you the slip, don't try to fake your reports. Bertha's too smart to fall for that. Good night, lover."

I heard the phone click at the other end of the line.

Over at the telephone desk, the girl slipped a movie magazine out from a drawer in her table, and began reading. The clerk kept on working with the books. No one seemed to have seen me go in. It was warm in the telephone booth, cold out in Bertha Cool's agency car, so I stayed in the telephone booth.

Two or three times during the next fifteen minutes, the girl at the switchboard had work to do, but she never glanced in my direction. So I sat on the uncomfortable stool in front of the telephone, and waited.

The two firemen came out. One of them seemed to be pretty confident. The other looked nervous. The girl at the switchboard glanced up. They didn't look at her, but went on out. I had the dope on their car, so I stayed put.

I figured I'd holed up in that booth long enough, and was just on the point of leaving, when the elevator door opened, and my man and the blonde came out.

The girl at the telephone desk looked up then. She looked at Cunner, then looked at the blonde. The blonde looked at her. The girl at the telephone desk looked away.

Cunner and the blonde started toward the door. I dropped my dime back in my pocket and had my hand on the brass handle on the inside of the folding glass door when Cunner turned suddenly on his heel and started back to the telephone desk.

The glass door was open just enough so I could hear him say, in a loud voice, "If any calls come in for me, I won't be back."

The blonde stood by the door. I could see the point of her chin tilted back over her shoulder. Her eyelids were drooping, and her eyes showed dark at the corners where they were turned as far as they'd go, looking over her shoulder at Cunner and the girl at the telephone desk—while keeping her face toward the night clerk.

Cunner's hand rested for a moment on the little shelf which ran along the side by the telephone desk. His manner was curt and businesslike. He hesitated for just a fraction of a second, then turned and walked rapidly to join the blonde.

Where his hand had been resting on the shelf was folded piece of white paper. It looked as though it had been torn from a notebook.

When Cunner and the girl had passed through the front door and out into the night, the girl at the switchboard shot out a smooth, white hand, and her tapering fingers closed hungrily over the piece of paper.

While she was reading the note, I left the telephone booth and walked rapidly to the lobby. The girl at the switchboard didn't see me. The night clerk looked up from his books to stare at my back. The back was all he saw.

It was raining outside, a cold drizzle which made the pavement on the highway a black ribbon reflecting the scattered light of houses nearby and the lights of occasional automobiles which hissed on by.

I sprinted for the agency heap as Cunner handed the blonde into his car.

I switched on the ignition, jiggled the choke back and forth, and pushed down on the foot throttle. The motor was cold. The bus caught, missed, backfired, and gave up the ghost.

I kept running the battery down while the red taillight on Cunner's automobile glowed into ruby brilliance—while it slid away from the curb in a graceful arc and disappeared in the distance down in the dark, tree-lined tunnel of Yucca City's main boulevard.

When I saw that the agency car didn't intend to do anything about it, I took my foot off the starter and waited for the battery to take a new lease on life. After twenty seconds, I tried again. Still no dice. It was a good two minutes after Cunner had driven away that the motor gave an apologetic cough, choked, sputtered, coughed again, and started hitting on about one cylinder. After a while, it picked up to two cylinders, and then suddenly roared into such rattling activity that raindrops scattered off the hood—as though the car had been a wet dog shaking itself.

Two minutes meant at least a mile and a half to Cunner's bus, and he'd gone away from there as though he'd been in a hurry. I looked at my wristwatch. It was eleven-thirty on the dot. I knew Bertha Cool would never believe that, so I made it eleven-thirty-one just to make it convincing, and chronicled the event. Then I shut off the ignition, turned up my coat collar against the rain, and went back to the apartment house.

Chapter III.

The night clerk looked up from his bookkeeping as I came in. I didn't look back at him, but I could feel his eyes following me all the way to the telephone desk.

I smiled at the girl at the switchboard. "Mr. Gell," I said. "Please tell him that Mr. Premmer sent me. He's expecting me."

"Mr. Gell's not in," she said.

I tried to put incredulity and disappointment on my map, and let her see the combination. "But he's expecting me."

"He's out."

"When will he be back?"

"I'm not certain he'll be back."

"Look here," I said, leaning over the wooden partition. "It's all right. You tell him Mr. Premmer sent me."

"But he's out," she said. And then, as she looked in my eyes, I saw her own soften. "Honest," she said, "he went out about ten minutes ago."

"Then he'll be back," I said confidently, "because he's expecting me."

She said, "He told me that if there were any messages, to say that he wouldn't be back again tonight."

I clung doggedly to the rail. "He'll be back. He's expecting me. Premmer sent me."

The night clerk looked over at the switchboard.

"Miss Marr," he called.

The girl looked up at him. He jerked his head. She took off her headset, swung out of the chair, and walked across to him.

He waited until she was close enough so his words would be inaudible to me. They talked together in low tones for a few seconds. She gave an unconscious gesture with her head in my direction so I knew they were talking about me. But the night clerk didn't look at me—not after that first look.

After a while, the night clerk went back to his books, and Miss Marr returned to the switchboard.

"I simply *have* to see him," I said. "Do you know where I could reach him with a telephone call or something?"

"No," she said, "I don't. I don't know where he went."

Her voice sounded thin and forlorn.

I lit a cigarette, puffed at it twice, then jerked it out of my mouth, and dropped it into the brass cuspidor.

"You can wait if you want to," she said, "but I'm quite certain he won't be back. He specifically told me so."

"He didn't say anything about me? Mr. Lam?"

"No."

I heaved a sigh. "Well," I said, "I know he'll be back. He'll get in touch with Mr. Premmer, and Premmer will tell him that I was on my way out. I was delayed, but Premmer told me to see him tonight."

"I don't think he'll be back," she said.

I paced the floor for a while, went over and sat down in a chair, then, when the night clerk started looking at me again, got up and walked over to the girl at the telephone desk. "Listen," I said in a low voice, "if he should call up, you be sure to tell him that Mr. Lam is waiting, won't you?"

"Okay, I will."

I hung around. "Nasty night out, isn't it?"

"Is it? It was clear when I came to work."

"I know, but clouds drifted in, and it started to rain. Maybe it's just a drizzle. What time did you come to work?"

"Four o'clock this afternoon."

An eight hour shift would make her time off at midnight.

I looked at my wristwatch, and said, so the night clerk would hear me, "Well, I'll wait until midnight. If he doesn't telephone by then, I'll have to call it off I guess. You're sure you don't know where I could reach him?"

"I haven't the faintest idea."

I stood there at the desk ostentatiously looking at my wristwatch. It was six minutes to twelve.

When the electric clock on the wall said two minutes of twelve, the girl at the desk started powdering her nose. She opened the drawer in the desk, took out the movie magazine, rolled it up, and snapped an elastic band around it.

"Well," I said dolefully, "I've got sixty seconds more, and then I guess I'm licked."

Her eyes showed sympathy.

At midnight, she clicked a few keys on the switchboard, slipped off the headset, went to the closet, and put on a baggy, cloth coat with imitation fox fur around the collar.

"You quitting?" I asked.

"Yes."

I said, "Well, I am too," and walked out toward the door. She was a dozen steps behind me. I heard her say goodnight to the night clerk, and his cold, toneless, "Good *morning*, Miss Marr."

It was raining hard outside. It was a cold rain. The drops were big and came down hard, making little bursts of water where they hit the dark pavement. I heard her give a little exclamation behind me as she saw the weather.

Yucca City turned out most of the lights at midnight. The clouds had settled low enough so the lights from the metropolitan district below were all blotted out. The Mountain Crest

Apartments seemed to be shut off from the rest of the world, an island of wan light isolated in a sea of darkness.

I looked back over my shoulder, and said, casually and taking care to keep eagerness from my voice, "Pretty wet. I have a car across the street. I'll give you a lift," and then added hastily, "that is, if you're going toward town."

She looked me over, and said, "I am. I didn't bring my galoshes. There wasn't a cloud in the sky when I came to work, and the paper said it was going to be clear today and tomorrow with seasonal temperatures."

"I know," I told her, and yawned to show that taking girls home after midnight came under the head of a chivalrous chore. "Wait here out of the rain, and I'll go get the crate—that is, if it'll start."

I sprinted through the rain, and prayed that Bertha Cool's idea of dependable transportation would do its stuff. It did.

I switched on the lights, started the windshield wiper, gunned the motor a couple of times, and skidded around in a U-turn.

I didn't get out when I drove up to the curb, but reached across and carelessly flung the door open. She ran across and jumped in beside me.

"Gosh, it's a cold rain," she said.

"Ain't it," I told her, and eased in the clutch. "Where do you go?"

The car lurched forward.

"Straight into Yucca City," she said. "It's about six blocks. You can let me off at the main intersection, and I'll walk up the hill."

"Okay," I said. As I slipped the car into second, I added, "I sure hated to miss Gell. It means a lot to me."

"I'm sorry," she said.

"This is a lonely place up here. Think you'd be afraid walking along this street after midnight."

"I am," she admitted. "It's pretty spooky, and the sidewalks haven't been cut through all the way. I don't mind it so much except in rainy weather. On clear nights it's beautiful. You can look out and see the lights of the city down below and the stars right above you. It looks," she went on wistfully, "as though you could take a good long jump and leave the whole world behind."

"You're too young to feel like that," I told her.

"You don't seem very chipper yourself—and you're young, too," she said.

I let that pass for a second. "What are those lights down the road?"

"The Yucca Club. They're trying to make a swanky nightclub out of it."

"Isn't this a funny place for a nightclub?"

"Not on clear nights," she said. "They have a swell place to dance."

"Dance," I said.

Her voice was wistful. "Uh huh. The floor is built out over the sidehill, on an enclosed porch. You dance out from the tables onto this porch and look down over the city lights. They keep it almost dark out there, just a starlight effect."

"It won't be starlight tonight," I said, "but a good shot of Scotch might help. How about it? Do you feel the same way about a slug of Scotch I do?"

She hesitated a minute, and said, "I don't know."

The main intersection loomed up, and I shot on past it.

"That was my street," she said.

I put on the brakes, and the agency bus skidded for a few feet, straightened, and skidded again. I felt her hand grab at my shoulder.

"It's okay," I said. "Tire a little smooth, that's all."

"Don't stop so quickly," she said.

"I won't," I told her, coasting along into the curb. "Can you make a U-turn in the middle of the block here, or do they put strangers in jail?"

"Better go to the next intersection," she said.

I looked along toward the lights of the Yucca Club. "We could," I suggested, "go in there and get just one slug of Scotch."

I felt her leaning toward me, her voice almost low-pitched in its eagerness. "Listen," she said, "did you want to see Mr. Gell *very* badly?"

"Did I!" I echoed.

"Listen, he *may* be there in the club. He likes to hang out there."

"That's swell. But I won't know him when I see him."

"I could point him out to you."

"Think he'd want to talk business at night?"

"I don't know," she said, fighting to keep her voice casual. "But we could find out if he's there."

"Yes," I said. "We could look in. The kind of business I have with him, I wouldn't want to discuss if he— Well, you know, if he was on a party."

"Well, we could see."

"Think he'd be alone?"

"Perhaps."

The windshield wiper was out of adjustment. It didn't scrape much rain off the windshield, but distributed the water in a half circle of distorted visibility. There were a couple of leaks where the windshield joined the body, and I could feel water dripping in on my right ankle. I said, "Look here, I don't mind spending dough when I get some action for it. But I don't like to blow what little money I have pretending I'm a millionaire when I'm not. Do they stick you in this joint?"

"Plenty," she said, "but— Oh, let's go in. I have a little money if you're short."

I looked at her and asked, "You want to go in that particular place for some particular reason?"

"Yes," she said, shortly.

"Okay," I said. "What's your first name?"

"Ruth."

"Mine's Donald," I said. "Donald Lam."

She said, "They don't have a cover charge, but there's a minimum. I think it's two dollars. If I pay for it, would you—would you go in and sit at a table with me and eat a dinner? They have a dollar and a half dinner that's very good, and we could sort of kill time and— You dance, don't you?"

"Uh huh."

"Well, we could dance and wait around until the place closes at two o'clock. You see, Donald, I can't very well go in without an escort and—and I want—I want to be having a good time if anyone should see me."

"You think we'll find Gell there?" I asked.

"Maybe."

"Okay, Ruth, let's go."

I turned into the circular driveway in front of the place. The attendant came forward with an umbrella. He looked down his nose at the car, but helped Ruth Marr out. I got out, and he gave me a celluloid check with a number on it. As a doorman swung open the main door for us, I saw the parking attendant looking at Bertha's car as though he hesitated about getting in and trying to drive the heap. Ruth Marr said, in a quick burst of conversation, "Let's go into the cocktail bar first, have a cocktail, and then go in and get a table. —Listen, Donald, please don't look as though we're—you're looking for anyone. Just pretend that you're with me, and that we're making a little whoopee, and—well, you know, that you're glad to be with me."

"Sure," I said.

She put her head up and sailed into the joint as though she was Mrs. Astor's pet horse. She tilted her chin a little bit, and gave me a seductive, sidelong glance and a low, throaty laugh as we stopped before the checking desk.

For a moment, the resemblance was startling. She'd been watching that blonde of Cunner's, and she must have been practicing the trick in front of a mirror.

The girl at the checking stand took my wet hat and Ruth's limp cloth coat while she sized us up with calculating eyes that failed to register any smile of greeting.

I took Ruth's arm, and led her into the hilarious gayety of the cocktail bar.

We sat at one end so we could look down along the bar. I tried to classify the different types. There were young men trying to look important; important men trying to look young. There were women of the brittle type who lavished passionate glances on their escorts and then, when the man raised his glass, hurriedly glanced around to see if some more likely looking sucker might be giving them the once over. There were women in pairs who were getting a little too loud; women who continually pawed over their men, men who kept making little gestures which brought their hands in contact with the bare backs of the women with them. Here and there, a couple who were evidently married to each other and were trying to recapture some of the lost spirit of courtship were getting more and more bored with each drink—and each other. Three bartenders were lazily engaged in mixing and serving drinks. They were studies in white-coated impassivity.

Gell and the blonde weren't there.

Ruth became anxious to get the drinks over with, and get into the main dining room.

I'd sold her on the idea of Scotch, but we changed to Bacardis when the bartender came to take our orders. We wrapped ourselves around the drinks, and Ruth was sliding off the stool almost before I had the last of my cocktail out of my glass.

We went to the door of the main dining room. As we entered, she tucked her hand under my arm, and looked up into my face with a blonde expression. Seductive laughter oozed from her lips. Two seconds later she'd turned from me to stare in an anxiety of hard-eyed dread around the dining room.

The headwaiter sized us up, and piloted us to an obscure table over in one corner. There was no one behind us. From our corner table, we could look out over the entire dining room.

I didn't need to ask her if Gell was there. Her roving eyes checked the tables behind me, and I could see an expression of relief flood her face as she completed the survey.

"You don't see anything of Gell, do you?" I asked, casually.

"No," she said. "He doesn't seem to be here—yet."

I was seated facing the long plate-glass windows which, on clear nights, commanded a view of the city below, but now were a dead black with rivulets of cold water trickling in aimless zigzags down the outer surface.

A waiter took our orders. Two dinners with no drinks.

"Let's dance," she said.

We went out on the floor. She was light on her feet. With my arm around her waist I could feel the ripple of smooth muscles beneath her clothes. Her firm breasts came close to me as we picked up the beat of the music and pushed into the crowd.

People mashed us, jostled us, trampled us. A middle-aged man, looking mighty proud of himself, danced by with a woman half his age, who rubbed and wiggled. A couple who were no longer young were trying all of the fancy steps, mostly on the toes of the other dancers. We were pushed over to a corner, where a party of sixteen sitting sedately at a table nearby evidently represented a meeting of some business organization. The men all seemed to know each other pretty well, while the women were more stiff and constrained, ranging from the frigid respectability of the executives' wives down to the good-looking bride of the young salesman who was so painfully anxious to make a good impression on everyone. Then the human whirlpool sucked us into its center once more.

We danced, and more people jostled against us, sending us in turn jostling against others. The couple who were hilariously doing the fancy steps bore down on us like a state highway truck on a construction job hogging the middle of the road. I piloted Ruth out of their way.

After a while, the music quit.

"You're some dancer, Ruth," I said.

She gave a nervous little laugh and squeezed my arm. "You, Donald, dance divinely—but you don't seem to get much pleasure out of it."

I looked in her eyes. "I'm just a little bit worried," I said. "It'll wear off after that drink begins to take effect and we have another dance."

We went back to the table. She put her purse on the corner within a few inches of my elbow. I knew that in that purse was the note Cunner had written to her. I knew that a man who measured up to Bertha Cool's standards of a good operative would be able to get that note out long enough to read it.

My job became distasteful to me. I wanted to get up and leave.

Looking out at the rain-lashed darkness, I felt Ruth's eyes on my face. I shifted my eyes quickly and caught hers. She met my stare steadily and frankly. "Donald," she asked, "why are you so cynical? You're too young to be like that."

"Cynical?" I asked. "I didn't know that I was."

"You are."

"What makes you think so?"

"The way you look. There's something bitter and disillusioned about you and about the way you look at people."

"I've lived long enough," I told her, "to know that people have to be taken with a pinch of salt."

She laughed. "You're salting them down in brine. Why be like that, Donald?"

"I don't know," I told her. "Let's dance, and this time keep your mind on me."

"Wasn't I before?"

"No."

"Well, after all," she said, "some of the responsibility rests on the man."

I took her up at that, and that next dance she didn't have a chance to think of anyone else. At first, she didn't like it, and then she did. After the music stopped and we'd started back to the table, she slipped her hand through the curve of my elbow, and said softly, "Really, I'm letting you do things that I wouldn't permit from anyone else unless I'd known him a long, long time—Donald, there's something fascinating about you."

"What?" I asked.

"I don't know," she said. "You're detached and cool and self-reliant—you're like a piece of steel that will bend easy but springs back into shape and is capable of taking a keen cutting edge."

"You," I told her, "must have been studying metals."

She laughed and said, "Not much, just a magazine article about the temper of things. Steel that's tempered too hard is worse than steel that's not tempered at all. Donald, do something for me, will you?"

"What?"

"How well do you know Gell?"

"I've never met him."

"I know, but you know a lot about him. You know what he's doing—and what you wanted to see him about?"

"Well?" I asked.

"Tell me," she said, leaning forward, "is that his sister, that blonde who's with him?"

"What blonde?"

"She's supposed to be his sister."

"What's her name?"

"Anita."

"What's the matter? Doesn't she act like his sister?"

Ruth Marr toyed with her water glass, the tips of her fingers twisting the glass around and around. Her eyes refused to meet mine. "No," she said, "she doesn't."

"Want me to find out for you?"

"Would you, Donald?"

"I might try, but it would be dangerous if Gell thought I was snooping."

"I know, Donald, but you could find out easily."

"It won't be so easy. Gell plays 'em close to his chest. He isn't an easy guy to check up on."

"Are you," she asked, "telling me?"

"What's the matter?" I wanted to know. "He been making passes at you?"

"No, no. He's just a tenant there in the building, and he's always nice to me. He has a nice voice over the telephone."

"Many calls?" I asked casually.

"Not many. They're always to that sister of his."

"What do they talk about?" I asked.

"You can't tell. It's sort of a code—" She broke off and said, "I just hear a word or two now and then. I wouldn't listen."

I kept my eyes on hers. She laughed nervously, and said, "Oh, all right. I listen in—and the more I listen, the less I know."

"I'll see what I can find out," I said.

We had a little food, and then the dance music started again. I looked at her inquiringly, and she nodded. That time, when we danced, I forgot about Bertha Cool, Mrs. Atterby, and Edith Cunner. I thought only of Ruth Marr. I could feel her body against mine. She was dancing close, and so was I. There wasn't anything vulgar about it, just her warmth mingling with mine and making me tingle all over. I suppose we were both lonesome and had been kicked around just enough so we clicked.

After that dance, I don't know where the time went. We talked and danced, and during one of the waltzes slid out into a dark corner of the porch, and I felt her trembling lips in a hot circle around my mouth.

I took her home when the place closed. It was raining cats and dogs. She lived in a house up on the hill a couple of blocks above the main drag. The hill was steep enough so one side of the house rested on the ground, and the downhill side was high enough so there was room for a little apartment. Ruth lived in that apartment.

She didn't go in right away. She said, "I'll say good night to you in the car, Donald, because the people upstairs sleep right over my door."

I said good night to her.

She didn't try to stop me in anything I did. I didn't try to do too much. I felt that if I did, it might spoil things. She let my hands wander around over the outside of her clothes, caressing her curves. I had a feeling that she'd given me the key to the city, but I didn't try any doors that I thought she'd prefer to keep locked.

It was almost half an hour later when she breathed, "Donald, darling, I simply *have* to go. I think you're awfully nice. Tell me, honey, where can I—when am I going to see you again?"

"I'll try to give you a ring sometime tomorrow."

"I don't know a thing about you, Donald," she laughed, "where you work, or what you do, or where you live, or—"

I tore a piece of paper from my notebook and scribbled the telephone number of my rooming house. "You can always reach me there," I said, "although sometimes I'm out for a day or two at a time, and I'm nearly always out evenings."

She started to ask me what I did, then decided that she'd wait for me to tell her, said, "Good night, Donald," and we kissed again.

It was still raining, and water had dripped through the cowl of the agency car and soaked my right foot. There was water running down over the rubber mat on the floor, but I was throbbing with warmth. I could feel her heart going pound—pound—pound—pound under the thin silk of her blouse. When I touched her cheeks, they were hot.

"Don't get out, Donald," she said. "I don't want you to. Just let me make a dash for it."

She opened the car door, slid out to the driveway, and ran up to the door of her little apartment. I sat there watching until she had unlocked the door, gone inside, and switched on the lights. Then I took off the brake, let the car coast downhill, slipped it into gear, and started it by gravity.

The rain was lashing against the windshield, showing as a wall in front of the headlights.

Chapter IV.

Bertha Cool was in her office when I showed up about ten o'clock. Elsie Brand looked up from her typewriter long enough to say, "Go on in. She wants to see you," and then resumed her perpetual hammering away at the keyboard.

I walked on in.

Bertha Cool was sitting at her desk. A long, carved ivory cigarette holder, stained a deep yellow from countless smokes, was held in the diamond-encrusted fingers of her right hand. She wasn't smoking seriously, just letting smoke seep through her nostrils. Her eyes were fastened on distance.

She looked up at me when I entered and said, "Hello, Donald. Sit down. Got a report?"

I handed her the typewritten sheet.

She read through the report. I waited for the sarcastic comment which would come when she had read about my failure to get the car started.

It didn't come.

She put the typewritten sheet down on her desk, and stared at me for a minute or two without seeing me. Then she said, "I've checked the registration on his car, Donald. It's in the name of A. L. Gell. He has a space in the garage under that name."

I nodded.

She said, musingly, "Donald, my love, I think you're a good mascot."

I didn't say anything.

"Wouldn't it be nice if Bertha Cool could cut herself a piece of cake, Donald?"

I didn't think that called for an answer. She didn't seem to expect any. She drifted off into a brown study, and after a while I took out a cigarette and lit it.

"Donald," she said, at length, "where's that crate of ours?"

"Downstairs in the parking lot."

She said, "Drive it around to the new car agency on Thirty-Second Street. They gave me the best trade-in allowance. You didn't fill the gasoline tank, did you?"

I shook my head.

"Don't. They have a demonstrator they're letting me have at a good price, and we don't want to give those sons of bitches any free gasoline. The deal's all made."

"A new car?" I asked in surprise.

"Uh huh."

"For agency business?" I insisted incredulously.

"You can use it on this case, Donald. Christ, we can't let a bunch of jack slip through our fingers because the bird we're tailing has a car that'll whisk right out from under our noses—and here in your report you say you lost out because our heap wouldn't start in the rain."

I tried to find a clue to this change of heart. "Did you," I asked, "look up Premmer?"

She heaved a deep sigh which came from down below her waistband. "Listen, Donald, darling, Bertha has been busy this morning. Bertha did a hell of a lot of thinking. We've not only looked up Premmer, but we've checked on the firemen and officers who were out. Donald, why in the hell didn't you get the dope on those speed cops?"

"I didn't know who they were going to see when they drove up," I said. "After all, it's a big apartment house."

She nodded, almost absently. Her cigarette burned down to the last quarter inch until it threatened to crack the end of the cigarette holder. Bertha took a long last drag, then picked up a hairpin on the desk and gouged out the burnt end of the cigarette. Bertha Cool didn't believe in wasting things. You could always tell her butts because they were burnt down to the last eighth of an inch. She fished for another cigarette, pushed it in the holder, but didn't light it immediately. She turned her cold, gray eyes toward me, and said, "You know, Donald, there's lots of money to made out of politics—if you get in on the ground floor."

She lit her cigarette then, inhaled a deep drag, and said, "You know, lover, it takes dough to keep new automobiles, beautiful blondes, and apartments out in Yucca City."

"Listen," I said, "if Cunner's mixed up in politics and wants to talk with city employees, why doesn't he do it? Why should he go to all the trouble of getting a blonde 'sister' and an apartment?"

Her eyes looked me over. "That's what I have you for, Donald."

"For what?"

"To find out the answer."

"Then what?" I asked.

"Politicians," she said, almost dreamily, "don't like private detective agencies. If you were a taxpayer and wanted to get information about what was going on, you'd have a hell of a time doing it, Donald. The politicians have passed laws licensing private detectives. Of course, they're not supposed to withhold or revoke licenses for political reasons, but there are lots of ways of killing a cat. Even before they had that law, politicians were powerful enough so most private detective agencies had to protect themselves by advertising they wouldn't tackle political investigations.

"They pretend it's because they don't want that class of business. The real truth is they're afraid to tackle it. There's no money investigating the politicians who are out of power. No one gives a damn about them. It's only after a politician gets in power that he needs investigating."

"Leading up to what?" I asked.

"Leading up to the fact that Bertha Cool isn't afraid of anything on God's green earth," she said. "I'll tackle anything there's money in. There's money in politics—if you play it right."

"And we're going to play it right?" I asked.

"Yes, Donald, darling, we are. And it's dangerous as hell. People who know too much have a habit of getting bumped off by gangsters. The police gird up their loins and make a lot of newspaper talk about how the gangsters can never invade their city. The police promise they're going to make arrests. They haul in a lot of gangsters for questioning. A lot of other gangsters leave town because they don't want to be questioned, and the police make a big stink over that. They broadcast a description of the gangsters, and the public thinks something's going to happen pretty pronto.

"It never does. After a while something else crowds the murder off the front page. Whenever news gets dull, the reporters come back to resurrect the murder case. The officers always have plenty of stuff to give them. Then, after a couple of months, it's history, and newspapers aren't concerned with history."

"I know *some* of the facts of life," I said.

She said, "Think *those* facts over, darling, because they're important. You might even be the corpse. You wouldn't want to be found in an alley with your body full of slugs, would you?"

"Not particularly."

"Well, darling, that's what's going to happen if you don't watch your step. It's why Bertha is getting you a nice new car with hydraulic brakes and lots of pickup. It's dangerous, Donald, and you and I are going to do the whole thing between us. We're not going to have any other operatives in on the play."

I began to see the sketch.

"Meaning, I suppose, that I'm going to be on the job day and night."

She looked at me long enough to nod and wait for me to say something.

I didn't say it. There was no use.

"If there's cake being passed around, my love, Bertha wants a big slice. I can trust you, Donald. You're a little runt, and you can't take a beating, and God knows you can't dish one out. But you have guts, and you're a cool customer in a pinch. You know how to keep your mouth shut.—Tell Elsie Brand to come in here."

I stepped to the door and motioned to Elsie Brand. She came in, bringing a shorthand book.

Bertha Cool said, "Take this report, Elsie, for Mrs. Atterby."

Elsie Brand sat down, crossed her knees, propped her notebook into position, saw me looking at her legs, pulled her skirt down, and waited for dictation.

Bertha Cool took my report and started dictating.

" 'Subject left place of business at seven minutes past five. Rented a car from a drive-yourself agency, and picked up unidentified blonde. Made a round of three or four nightclubs, dancing and drinking. Did not change into evening clothes. Blonde is girl about twenty-seven, wearing expensive clothes with good figure, and what operative describes as swell legs. After leaving last nightclub, subject drove at high speed toward town. It was raining and operative tried to follow, but was arrested for speeding. Before he could square things enough to get underway, subject had vanished. Operative has good description of blonde, and expects to locate her definitely tonight.' —That's all, Elsie."

Elsie Brand silently took her book and retired to the outer office.

Bertha Cool beamed at me. "No use giving them too damn much information all at once," she said. "And, after all, we don't want Mrs. Atterby busting into the picture with divorce proceedings and killing the little goosie that's going to lay the nice golden eggs for Bertha, do we, Donald, my love?"

"It seems like a hell of a report to me," I said. "We should at least give her the license number of the automobile, or show that we've checked up on the name under which it was rented from the drive-yourself agency."

Bertha Cool narrowed her eyes thoughtfully.

"Mrs. Atterby," I went on, "isn't exactly a fool, and she has a suspicious nature."

Bertha nodded. "All mother-in-laws do," she said. She picked up the telephone on her desk, and said to Elsie Brand, "We'll change that report, Elsie. We won't say that he picked up the car at a drive-yourself agency. We'll say he entered a car which was parked at a garage half a dozen blocks from his office, and we'll give them the license number of the car."

She hung up the telephone and turned to me. "Even if they investigate," she said, "they'll only find a lead to A. L. Gell, and that won't mean anything."

Bertha Cool turned back to consult my report. She studied it for a moment or two, then looked up at me and said, "Donald, what about this switchboard girl?"

"Ruth Marr?"

"Yes."

"Well, what about her?"

"I don't like the way this report reads," she said. "You say that Cunner came out and gave her a note. Subsequently, you got acquainted with her, and drove her home—'stopping in for a drink and a bite but not getting any information.'"

She looked up at me with hard, suspicious eyes.

"What's wrong with that?" I asked.

"Everything."

When I didn't say anything, she went on, after a moment, "You're trying to protect her, Donald. You want her kept out of it. Now ordinarily she would have been your best lead for getting information. Even an amateur would know that. You brought her into the picture all right, and then you broke your neck easing her out. You know, Donald, that's your big trouble. You fall in love every time you fall for a jane. You shouldn't do that. If a girl looks good to you, go on the make. Love her where you find her, and leave her where you love her.

"Christ, Donald, it's just a biological urge—or should be. But it isn't normal with you. And yet that's why some women go nuts over you. If you'd only get the right attitude toward women, you could go a long ways in this business. When a woman gives you everything, she kicks through with *all* she has. You could get a hell of a lot of information for Bertha if you'd play it right. But, no, you won't do that. You fall in love with some little floozy, and put her on a pedestal, and let your manly instinct of protection cover her with a mantle. Christ, Donald, it isn't natural!

"Now, here's what I want you to do, Donald, my love. Go out and cultivate this Ruth Marr. Take her to the races this afternoon. Go on the make for her, and don't be wishy-washy about it. Go right after her, and—"

"Thanks," I said. "I don't need any suggestions as to how to spend my spare time."

She heaved a deep, tremulous sigh, and said, "Donald, you're the most obstinate little bastard I ever saw. After all Bertha's done for you, too! You won't lift a finger to help Bertha."

I said nothing.

She said wearily, "Oh well, go on down to the agency and trade this car in. Ask for Mr. Smith. He's the one who made the deal, and go through the old car, Donald, dear, and take out every goddamn thing we can use. There are two pairs of pliers in there, and I think an extra screwdriver, and don't forget the flashlight in the glove compartment. When you get the new car, be sure there are plenty of tools in it. Don't let those bastards shortchange you on a thing. Then drive it out to your rooming house and park it on the shady side of the street. Mind you now that you don't leave it in the sun, and don't go driving it around on your own business. You keep a record of every mile that goes through that odometer while you're driving the car."

I got up and started for the door.

"Donald," she called, as I had my hand on the knob.

I turned.

"Take a look at the gas tank on our car. If there's more than a couple of gallons in it, get a can and drain it out. You'll find a drain plug in the bottom of the tank."

I said, "Okay," and opened the door.

"Donald."

"Yes."

"Be sure they give you a full tank of gas with that new car. They're supposed to do it, you know, and those sons of bitches will chisel you at every turn of the road if you give them a chance."

"Yes," I said, and went out.

Chapter V.

Mr. Smith at the car agency looked at my heap with a jaundiced eye.

"The Bertha Cool car," I said by way of explanation.

He stared at the car once more. Then he said, "She told me the make and model all right, but I made the deal on the strength of the car being in good condition. This needs a paint job, tires, work done on the motor, and there's a leak in the radiator."

I lit a cigarette and said, "That's out of my department. I'm in the delivery department."

"What's your telephone number up at the agency?"

I told him.

He strode into the office. Through the plate-glass window I could see him jerk a receiver out of its cradle, place it to his ear, and jab a stubby forefinger into the dial holes. He spun the dial furiously.

After the first few seconds, his jaw quit working. I saw him wilt down inside his shirt. After a while, he began to nod his head. Then he tried a sickly smile, and made as though to hang up. But Bertha wasn't letting him off that easy. He tried twice more to get the conversation ended, but it was no soap. When he finally got the receiver back on the hook, the only thing he'd said in the last five minutes had been accompanied by nods of the head.

He came on out, looking a couple of inches shorter than when he went in. "Okay, buddy," he said. "You're to take the new bus."

"Uh huh."

He led me over to it. Halfway over, he said, "This Bertha Cool is a card all right."

"Card, hell," I told him, "she's the whole deck."

He looked at me and started to laugh, but it was a laugh that didn't have much mirth in it.

I got the car, saw that I wasn't chiseled on the tools, made them fill it to the brim with gasoline, checked the oil, made them test the battery, and then drove it out.

It was a dream, a sweet, smooth-running car that made no more noise than a sewing machine and jumped like a greyhound when I put my foot on the throttle. I figured Cunner would have a hell of a time ditching me in *that* bus.

At four-thirty I set the trip odometer back to zero, put my notebook on the seat beside me where it would be handy, and went out to Webley & McMarr.

I had a hunch Bertha Cool hadn't spent the day sitting down twiddling her fingers or letting grass grow under her feet, but she hadn't seen fit to tell me what she was doing, and I didn't particularly want to know.

Cunner came out at six minutes past five. After having followed him the night before, it was a cinch to pick him up out of the crowd. He was tall enough to send his green felt hat bobbing along well above the heads of the others, and his tweed overcoat, in a raglan cut across the shoulders, gave him a long, loose-jointed appearance of easy power as he walked.

He walked over to the same car line and climbed aboard a car. I was so certain he was going to get off at the garage and pick up the Gell automobile that I loped along behind mechanically, debating with myself whether I should speed ahead of the car in order to—

I had to slam on my brakes suddenly when the car stopped

abruptly at the corner. Cunner swung off the car steps, and walked directly across the street to a parking lot.

I pulled in to the curb too close to the intersection and in a red zone. I prayed that no cop would come along until I saw what it was all about. My best bet was that he was dropping in to talk with someone about a business deal.

Two minutes later he came out, driving a car which looked so much like the agency heap I'd turned in that morning that I couldn't be certain for a moment it wasn't the same one. It wasn't, but it was a good imitation.

He wheezed and jolted along through the traffic, coaxing the car into slow motion at the intersection after the signals changed, backing it into lopsided acceleration between blocks, squeaking it to protesting stops at the red signals. I purred along behind, riding the brakes about half the time to keep from climbing over his back bumper.

This time he didn't take the north boulevard, but turned over to the west, and then went south. He wound up in a cheap apartment district, parked the car in front of a rather frowzy, three-storied brick apartment house, and went in.

I parked my car where it wouldn't be too conspicuous, and sat waiting for Cunner to come out.

He didn't come out.

It got dark, and I got hungry. The day had been clear, but the night was turning cold, and this was a low section of town where the damp air clung to the ground like a blanket.

I looked up and down the street and didn't see anything which looked like a place to eat.

I compromised on a cigarette, huddled down inside my thin overcoat, and tried to hug warmth into myself.

Lights came on and went off in the apartment house.

People came and went. None of them was the man I wanted. I kept getting more and more hungry.

A speed cop came roaring up on his motorcycle. He over-shot the apartment house, slowed down half a block up the street to look for numbers, then leaned way over as he made a U-turn in the middle of the block and came back. He kicked the prop under his motorcycle and went into the apartment house.

I went over and noticed the license number.

He came out ten minutes later, and I kicked myself for not having made a quick run for a sandwich while he was there.

About seven-ten a car with a tax-exempt license plate drove up in front of the apartment house. Two men got out and went in.

I ran across, noticed the license number, sprinted back, stepped on the starter, and sent Bertha Cool's new car zipping down the street. I had to go six blocks to a through boulevard before I found a café. A sleepy-eyed man behind the counter didn't see any reason why he should hurry, or his customers should do likewise. I gulped coffee while he was making a leisurely job of cooking a hamburger. Even the stove wasn't more than lukewarm, and took its time about the cooking.

When he handed me the sandwich, I grabbed it, slid twenty cents across the counter, and sprinted out to Bertha Cool's car.

I drove with one hand and ate hamburger with the other, and I wasn't driving anywhere near the legal limit. I got to the apartment house, slid the car to a stop, switched off the lights, took a satisfying bite of the hot meat and steamy bread soaked with its meat juices—and then suddenly quit chewing, my jaw half open.

Cunner's car was gone. So was the car with the tax-exempt license plate.

I knew how Bertha Cool would feel about that. I'd lost the guy the night before, but I had an alibi then. I could blame it on the car. Now Bertha Cool had bought a new car so I could be sure to keep him in sight, and I'd let him slip through my fingers.

I looked at my watch. It was seven-twenty-one. I could stall off calling Bertha Cool until eight o'clock—perhaps until eight-thirty. But she'd be sure to ask the details as to when I'd lost him.

I decided it shouldn't interfere with my taking on nourishment, so I finished the sandwich, wiped my hands on my handkerchief, then climbed out of the car, and walked over to the apartment house.

The lobby was a T-shaped wide place at the front end of the corridor. An uncomfortable wicker settee and chair had been wedged into the place. It was illuminated by a reddish light which couldn't have been much over ten candlepower. I saw a sign on the door of apartment one, and, without bothering to strain my eyes reading it, took it for granted it said "MANAGER."

I knocked on the door.

After a while, a peroxide blonde of about thirty-five opened the door and surveyed me with eyes that were hard and cynical, a mouth that was ready for a smile only if I proved to be a cash customer. Otherwise, she seemed poised to give me the bum's rush.

"You have any vacancies?" I asked.

"Single, double, or bachelor?" she asked.

"Bachelor."

"No."

"I might consider a single."

"Thirty-seven-fifty."

"On the north or south side?"

"North."

"Get any sun?"

"Of course. Every apartment in the place gets sunlight."

"Let's look at it," I said.

She looked me over and decided I might be a cash customer after all. Her lips twisted into a smile. "What," she asked, "was the name?"

"Sinclair," I said. "Robert Sinclair."

"This way," she told me. She took a passkey from a hook just inside the door, and led the way down the corridor, bored but businesslike, and masking her hard voice behind a synthetic cordiality of manner. "Just yourself?" she inquired.

"I may have someone rooming with me," I said. "Funny thing how I happened to come here. A man whom I haven't seen for years—used to work with the Southern California Edison Company. Heck of a nice chap. His name's a short one, and hanged if I can place it. —Say, by the way, you may be able to help me out. He recognized me instantly, called me by name, and I hate to tell him I can't remember his. He's a tall man around thirty-five with wavy, chestnut hair and a straight nose. He has some trouble with his teeth, and his chin doubles back. The boys in the office used to call him Andy Gump—behind his back, of course. It used to make him sore as thunder." I laughed slightly and said, "That's the way a man's mind plays tricks on him. When I saw him, I immediately thought of Andy Gump, and that was the only name I could bring to my mind."

"I guess you mean Ned Pines in 208."

"Pines!" I exclaimed. "That's the chap. I wonder if the boys still call him Gump."

She laughed. "I wouldn't know." She paused before the door of an apartment and opened it.

I walked on in and looked around. It was a dark dump on the ground floor on the north side. A two-story building on the north was separated from it only by the width of a driveway.

"Where," I asked, "does the sun come in?"

"Right here," she said, taking me into a kitchenette and showing me a half window over the sink, a window about as big as a framed picture. "The sun just streams in here during the mornings."

The window was on the north side, but through it you could see past the corner of the other house. There was an opening between it and the garage. In the summer, when the sun was farthest north, the window probably got half an hour of early morning sunlight.

I looked the place over a little dubiously. "It's not exactly what I was looking for. You don't have anything on the south?"

"Not during the winter," she said. "During the summer I have lots of them. Now this apartment is one of the most desirable in the whole place. It's quite livable the year around. You don't have to move out in summer."

"Yes," I said, "that's true. Well, I won't ask you to save it, but if it isn't rented by tomorrow evening, I'll bring a friend to look at it. There's some chance we may double up."

"Very well, Mr. Sinclair."

The apartment smelled as though it had been vacant for months. She seemed as glad to get out of it as I was.

We walked back down the corridor in silence. She'd showed the apartment and done her duty. She knew as well as I did that it was a lemon.

I told her good night and went out to the car and did a little more thinking. God, how I hated to call Bertha Cool.

I might as well be sunk as the way I was. It would take about half an hour to run out to Yucca City, and, anyway, I wanted to see Ruth. So I slid in behind the wheel and made time, keeping away from the center of town, dodging what traffic I could, and taking a chance on getting pinched.

The night clerk at the Mountain Crest Apartments didn't

seem at all glad to see me, and I bore up under the strain remarkably well. I walked across to where Ruth was seated at the switchboard. She flashed me a glad smile of recognition and gave me her hand. I held it until the night clerk's stare was as chilly as a cold shower on a foggy morning.

"Gell in?" I asked aimlessly.

"Yes," she said. "He came in about ten minutes ago."

"Alone?" I asked.

She avoided my eyes. "Uh huh."

She was reaching for a cord on the switchboard, and I said, "Wait a minute. Don't call him just now, Ruth. I'm supposed to call Premmer before I try to see him. Premmer said it was all right last night, but I haven't an okay for tonight."

I headed toward the booth. She said, in a low voice, "Go in booth 2, and I'll save you a dime, Donald."

I shook my head at her. "Thanks a lot, Ruth, but we have an audience." I jerked my head in the direction of the night clerk.

"Oh him," she said, in a tone that spoke volumes. But I was moving away from her as she spoke and ducked into the pay station.

I spent a dime and called Bertha Cool.

"Hello, Donald," she said. "What's new?"

"Lots," I told her. "Our man has another apartment and another car. This time he's Ned Pines. He's in 208 in the Orange Cove Apartments."

"Are you near there now, Donald?" she asked.

"No, I'm back out at Yucca City. He had a few more city employees call on him at the Orange Cove Apartments. Ned Pines' car doesn't amount to much. I could have followed it on roller skates."

"But what are you doing out at Yucca City, Donald?" she asked.

"I tailed him out," I said. "He left the Orange Cove about thirty or forty minutes ago, and came out here."

She thought that information over for a minute, then suddenly said, "How did he come out, Donald, in the dilapidated bus or in the Gell car?"

Damn her, she would have to ask that.

I hesitated a minute, and said, "The Gell Car," mumbling my words together. If it came to a showdown I could claim she'd misunderstood me, and I'd said the old car.

"Where did—"

I knew she was going to ask where he'd picked up the Gell car and what he'd done with the old one, so I interrupted to say, "Just a minute. I'll give you the license number on the wreck he's driving and the license numbers of the cars his visitors were driving."

I fished out my notebook and read off the numbers more rapidly than she could take them down. She said, "For Christ's sake, Donald, hold your horses. I'm not a shorthand operator. Now give me those again, and give them to me slow."

I read them off slowly, figuring that a little irritation would take her mind off some of the questions she'd been going to ask.

"Any visitors out at the Mountain Crest Apartments?" she asked, when I'd finished with the numbers.

"Not yet. He just got there."

"How did he arrange the switch in cars, Donald? What—"

"Just a minute," I interrupted. "I think he's coming out now. Someone in the elevator—G'bye."

I hung the phone up and mopped perspiration off my forehead. I went out of the telephone booth and said to Ruth Marr, "I've got to wait a while before I see him. I'm to get some more information from Premmer."

"Be back, Donald?" she asked.

I nodded.

She raised her eyebrows in a gesture, beckoning me over closer.

I walked over to lean against the little partition which separated the switchboard desk from the lobby. "Donald," she said, in a low voice, "I just wanted to tell you how much I enjoyed last night—this morning."

"Maybe you think I didn't."

"Did you really?"

"Uh huh."

"You're so nice, Donald," she said. "You—well, you must have known—I was lonesome—you didn't try to crowd things. Donald, I'm for you.—Tell me, honey, is she *really* his sister?"

"I can't tell you," I said, and then added significantly, "yet. Give me a little more time."

"Didn't Premmer know?"

"I'm not in a position to ask."

Her face grew hard. "Well," she said, "if you won't tell me, I'll tell you."

"What?"

"She isn't his sister."

"No?" I asked.

Her lips were in a firm, straight line, her voice vibrant with emotion. "I hate him," she said. "Oh, *how* I hate him!"

"What's the matter?"

"He's a married man."

"Married?"

She nodded and blinked back tears.

"How do you know, Ruth?"

She tried to say something, but couldn't talk. She shook her head as a sign she didn't want to talk about it. After a moment, she said, "You'll be back after a while, Don?"

I nodded.

"Have a talk with me," she said, "before—before you go up."

I leaned across the shelf. "Look here, Ruth. I don't want to do business with him if he isn't on the square. Tell me what you know."

"Oh, I guess he's all right so far as business is concerned. It's only—only—oh well, skip it."

"Now don't be like that, Ruth. I want to know. A man can't be crooked in his private life and honest in business, that is, if he can, he isn't."

She looked up at me. "Donald, can you tell me what you want to see Gell about, what kind of business—"

The night clerk said icily, "Miss Marr, I have a series of calls for you to make, a list of people whom I wish you to ring up. Will you come and get the list please?"

She flashed me a swiftly pleading look. I raised my voice and my hat at the same time, and said, "I'll be back in half an hour," and then, meeting the night clerk's eyes, said, "Try and save ten or fifteen minutes for me then."

I walked out.

I looked up and down the street and could find no sign of the old wreck that I'd trailed out to the Orange Cove Apartments. I walked on back into the garage and passed the time of day with the Swede janitor, telling him I thought I'd found a job, working for a wealthy Swedish couple, that it would be a swell job, that one of my parents had been Swedish, and I knew I'd get along swell.

The janitor listened to me but didn't say much. I went through the motions of looking around the place, ostensibly to see if I'd passed up any live bets the night before.

Gell's car wasn't there.

"That was a swell car I was looking at last night," I said. "Sure had lots of soup. Who was it that owned it—oh yes, Gell. He isn't in tonight, huh?"

The Swede said he hadn't come in yet and let it go at that.

I walked out and began to worry about that telephone call to Bertha Cool. I remembered what she'd said about trying to fake my report in case I lost him.

I sat out in the car, smoked a couple of cigarettes, and thought. The more I thought, the less I could figure out. The time element was just about right, and, of course, Gell could have ditched his old heap and taken a taxi to the apartment house. I stared moodily out through the windshield at the flow of traffic along the boulevard. I was in a spot, and it was a spot I didn't like.

A gray sedan pulled up to the curb. A thin figure, in a double-breasted, checkered suit, got out of the car, and then struggled into an overcoat with a high collar.

A person usually slips off his overcoat after he gets out of his car and before entering an apartment house. It isn't often the process is reversed. I watched the figure all the way into the apartment house, and then did some more thinking about my own problems. I decided I'd better ask Ruth Marr a couple of questions. She might be able to tell me how my man had arrived. At least, if he'd come in a taxi, the night clerk would know, and she could find out from the night clerk.

I got out of the car and crossed over to the lobby. I didn't see the night clerk at the desk, and figured that was a break for me. Someone was huddled over the switchboard—Ruth, as I thought. But when I had taken two steps toward the telephone desk something about the huddled figure struck my attention. I paused to stare as I recognized the shoulders of a man's coat.

I took it for granted it was the night clerk and turned around and beat it back to the car, noticing that Ruth was nowhere in sight.

After a while, the figure in the overcoat, the checkered suit, and hat pulled low over the forehead, emerged from the lobby, walked quickly to the gray sedan, and drove away. On general principles, I turned for a flash at the license number—just to see that it wasn't a county car. Beyond that, I paid no attention to it.

Four minutes later, I heard running steps on the sidewalk behind the car. It was a woman running. I turned to take a look, and saw Ruth Marr. She was carrying something in her right hand, something that glittered, and her face was frozen into a mask of terror.

She flashed me a swift glance from glassy eyes, started to run on past, and then suddenly checked herself.

"*Donald!*" she said, in a voice that sounded as though her mouth was dry.

"What is it, Ruth?"

"You didn't tell me you had a new car. I was looking—looking for the other one."

"You were looking for me?"

She nodded.

"What is it?" I asked.

She climbed into the car and sat down beside me.

"What's that in your hand, Ruth?" I asked.

She shook her head, refusing to meet my eyes. I slid my arm around her shoulders. She was trembling like a dead leaf in a breeze.

"Ruth," I said, "what is it?" and slid my hand down her arm, pulling her hand out into view. Then I switched on the dash-light, took a good look, and switched it back off.

"Thirty-eight caliber, Smith and Wesson police positive," I said. "What's the idea? Did you stage a holdup or something?"

She made a quick, convulsive half turn, flung her arms around my neck, and started to cry. I patted her shoulders, told her everything was all right, felt the tension of her quivering muscles, realized her tears were at the verge of hysterics.

I pushed her back and said, "Listen, Ruth, what the hell? Tell me about it."

"I c-c-can't."

"Don't kid me, and don't kid yourself, Ruth. Give me the dope. What is it?"

"I don't know."

"What *do* you know?"

"S-s-s-someone came out of Gell's room."

"What were you doing up there?"

"He—he—I wanted a showdown."

"What about?" I asked.

"About his being married. He's been stringing me along."

"Go on," I said. "What else?"

She said, "I asked Mr. Epsworth to relieve me for a few minutes. I told him I was ill."

"Epsworth," I said, "the night clerk?"

"Yes. George—George Epsworth."

"Go on," I said.

"I went out to the restroom, and then climbed the stairs to the second floor, and took the elevator to the sixth," she said. "As I started toward Arthur's apartment—"

"Gell's?" I interrupted.

"Yes. Arthur Gell. The other elevator car was there on the sixth floor, standing with the door hooked open. There's a hook on the door that the janitor uses when he's moving furniture so no one can take the elevator away from him. It's automatic, you know, and—"

"Yes, I know," I said. "What about it?"

"And Arthur's apartment is right across from the elevator

door. It's apartment six hundred. Well, when I was pretty close to the apartment, the door opened, and a funny man came out. He was wearing a big, black overcoat and had a checkered suit underneath it. A hat was pulled down over his face, and he— was carrying—this gun."

"Go on," I said, keeping my eyes away from hers.

"I don't know. I guess I screamed. Anyway, this man saw me. He threw the gun at me, right at my feet, jumped in the elevator, and unhooked the door."

"What did you do?"

"I ran to the elevator and kept jabbing the button, but it was no use. The elevator was on its way down, and you know the way it is with those elevators. One signal has to be completed before you can do anything with another."

"There were two elevators, weren't there?"

"Yes. I never thought about taking the other. I was too frightened. And then all of a sudden, I wondered what would happen if the elevator *did* come back up, and left me facing the burglar."

"Burglar?" I asked.

"Yes, of course. That's what he must have been doing in there."

"But Gell was in there, wasn't he?"

"Yes."

"Strange time for a burglar to pick."

"I know, Donald, but I'm telling you what I thought at the time."

"Go on. What happened after that? I suppose you're getting ready to tell me you picked up the gun."

"Yes," she said. "How did you know?"

"I'm just good at guessing," I said. "So you picked up the gun. Then what?"

"I picked it up and waited for the elevator to come back. You know, if you keep pressing the button quickly and the person in the elevator isn't wise to the trick, you can capture the elevator just the moment it hits the lower floor and before the person can get the door open. Once the door is open, that keeps the signal from making a contact and—"

"Yes, I know all about apartment house elevators. Go on. What did you do?"

"Well, I couldn't get the elevator back, and when it finally did come up from the ground floor, it was empty. So I knew the man had got away then, unless I could telephone the night clerk and get him to head him off."

"So what did you do?"

"So I ran into Arthur's apartment and grabbed up the receiver and—then—"

I waited for her to go on, sitting there keeping absolutely silent and keeping my eyes resolutely turned away from hers.

"Then," she said, "I saw—what was on the floor."

"Gell?" I asked.

"A man's legs, all sprawled out with the toes turned cock-eyed. He was half in the kitchen, and half in the living room. The half I saw was in the living room."

"Now let's see," I said. "You had the telephone at your ear. You were going to call the night clerk and tell him to head off the man in the overcoat and the checkered suit who was coming down in the elevator."

"Who had gone down in the elevator," she corrected. "The elevator had already stopped on the ground floor, and come back at my signal, but I figured George could catch him before he'd gone very far, or at least catch the automobile. —Well, when I suddenly saw those legs, I dropped the receiver back into place."

"And then what?"

'Then I thought of you, Donald. I knew you'd be sitting out here in an automobile somewhere, so I just dashed down the stairs in a blind panic."

"And brought the gun with you, I suppose?"

"Yes."

"Now let's get this straight, Ruth. Do you want me to believe that story?"

Her eyes grew wide and round. "Why, yes, of course. It's the truth."

"It doesn't sound like it."

I could see she was hurt. "*Donald*, I thought you were so nice. I thought you'd—understand."

"I do," I said. I shifted my position so I could look into her eyes. "Tell me again it's the truth."

Her eyes were close to mine. "It's the truth," she said, and then her quivering, salty lips were searching for mine, and my own cheek grew wet where her tear-streaked skin had been placed against mine. I fought against believing her as a drowning man fights to keep the water from closing over his head. Christ, I simply *couldn't* believe her. There was too much at stake for both of us. I had to know the truth and just what we were up against. Yet the minute her body came close to mine, I could feel my pulse start pounding. My hand slid down along her blouse and cupped around her right breast, without any conscious volition on my part. Her right arm stole quietly around my neck. She drew me to her, and I could feel her lips hot against mine.

Something heavy was pressing against my leg. I reached my hand down to move it. It was the gun.

The touch of that cold steel brought me back to earth.

"Listen, Ruth," I said, "if you killed him, for God's sake say so.

It's all right with me. I'm for you no matter what happens. All I want is the truth. I want to know what I'm up against. Tell me, darling, is that story you told me the truth?"

"So help me God, Donald, it's the truth."

I said, "One thing I want to know about. You were holding the telephone receiver to your ear—you looked in the living room and saw those two legs, is that right?"

"Yes."

"And then you put the receiver back?"

"Yes."

"You must have done something, must have said something. You must have—"

"I think I screamed."

"You *think* you screamed," I said, "into the telephone?"

"Yes, Donald. I—I—I guess I must have. I don't know."

"How did you get out?" I asked.

"Through the tradesmen's entrance into the alley."

"Go back through the tradesmen's entrance," I said. "Go into the restroom, powder your nose, wash your eyes in cold water. Go out and tell George you're feeling like the devil, but you'll try to stick it out. Sit there at the switchboard and take it. No matter what it is, take it right on the chin, and don't wince. And no matter what happens, remember that you left the switchboard and went to the restroom. You were feeling like the devil."

She laughed nervously, and said, "Do I have to go into details?"

"No," I said. "The cops know the facts of life."

She said shakily, "Oh, Donald, hold me. I feel so damn—"

I pried her arms from around my neck, and pushed her back. "Don't be a fool," I said. "Remember, except for that trip to the restroom, you haven't left the switchboard. Now get back there and take it, and if you break down and spill anything, you're going to get us both in a hole. Do you understand?"

"But, Donald, why can't I tell them the truth? Why can't I—"

"Listen, kid," I said. "I've fallen for you so bad it hurts. I believe you. But I won't believe you after you've left. I wouldn't believe your story if I read it in the papers. I wouldn't believe it if I were on a jury. This is once when the truth won't work. Get back there, away from me, and let me think."

"What are *you* going to do?"

"I don't know," I said.

"Oh, Donald, you do too! You're trying to make it easy for me. Tell me what you're going to *do*."

I jerked open the door of the automobile and climbed out. "I'm going to throw you out if you don't get started," I said.

She reached for me. I grabbed at her legs. She gave a nervous scream and kicked. I caught the right leg. She anchored her skirt between her legs by turning her right hand sideways and pushing it down tight between her thighs. I dragged her out.

She slid off the seat. I caught her to me. Her lips brushed my ear. "Donald," she said, "you *darling*." And then she was gone, running down the street toward the alley.

I stood there by the car looking with cynical eyes at the .38 Smith & Wesson revolver lying on the seat.

Chapter VI.

Gradually, in the cool night air, the symptoms of masculine emotion subsided, and that gun crowded the romance out of my mind. I thought back on Ruth Marr's story, and no more believed it than I had when she'd first told it and I'd been looking out through the windshield, avoiding her eyes. I felt as skeptical as the modern boy whose mother has just told him about how the nice stork brought the baby next door.

There I was, alone with the gun. Hell, I was in for it now. I'd made the play. I might as well get some of the sweet. I'd already signed up for the bitter.

I took a handkerchief from my pocket, went over to the front of the car, raised the hood, pulled out the oil gage, and got a few drops of oil on a corner of the handkerchief. Then, with the oiled rag, I went over that gun, covering every inch of it, scrubbing off all fingerprints. I found the gun's numbers and copied them into my notebook.

I swung out the cylinder and noticed there were six cartridges. One of them had been exploded. I pushed the cylinder back into place so the hammer was directly over that exploded cartridge. Then, holding the gun in the oiled handkerchief, I got out of the car and started exploring.

A block down the street from the Mountain Crest Apartments, I found a place where the sidehill had been slipping enough to crack the gutter. For a while, the authorities had patched it up by pouring hot asphalt into the cracks, but more cracks had opened up, and finally the county had let them go, evidently on the theory that the dry season wasn't far off and what difference did it make anyway. The real estate boom had collapsed, and no more property was being sold.

I explored around the cracks in the pavement until I found one that would just accommodate the gun. I put a little earth on top of it, tamped it down, then went back to the car. I wiped all the oil off my hands, put the handkerchief in the glove compartment, straightened my tie, and marched boldly into the Mountain Crest Apartments.

The night clerk stared steadily at me with eyes that were as cold as those of a dead fish. Looking him over, something about him struck me as being vaguely familiar—a something which I should have noticed. I was halfway to Ruth Marr's desk before it suddenly flashed across me what it was. He was wearing a checkered suit, almost identical in pattern with that worn by the person wearing the overcoat who had entered the apartment house.

Ruth Marr looked up as I approached the desk. Her eyes looked slightly swollen, but if I hadn't know what to look for, I probably wouldn't have noticed it. Her color was a little too vivid where she'd tried to gild the lily, but she managed a nice smile and said, "Hello, Donald. I see you're back."

"Yes," I said. "I want to see Mr. Gell. Give him a ring, will you, Ruth?"

"You mean Mr. Gell in six hundred?"

"I think that's his apartment. Tell him Mr. Lam is calling, that Mr. Premmer told me to give him a ring. —He's up there, isn't he?"

"Yes. He went up an hour or so ago, and hasn't gone out yet."

She smirked her lips into what was meant for a courteous smile, and snaked a line up from the switchboard and into a socket. A light flashed on the switchboard, and she started pressing a key. After a few seconds, she frowned, jiggled the connection, and did some more pressing on the key. Finally she turned and said, "That's strange. He doesn't answer."

I turned quickly toward the desk as I sensed someone quietly approaching. It was George Epsworth, the night clerk. "Who doesn't answer, Miss Marr?" he asked quietly.

"Mr. Gell."

"Isn't he up there?"

"Yes. He went in about an hour ago. He hasn't gone out—not that I know of. He didn't go out while I was—while you were at the board, did he?"

"No."

"Then he's in there."

And she rang the telephone again and again.

"Perhaps he isn't answering his telephone," I said, "doesn't want to be disturbed or something."

Epsworth said, "If that were the case, he certainly would have taken down his receiver to tell us to quit ringing. He's probably stepped out for a few moments into one of the other apartments. You'll have to wait, Mr.—what was the name?"

"Lam," I said. "Donald Lam."

"I'm afraid you'll have to wait, Mr. Lam. Do you have an appointment with Mr. Gell?"

"Not exactly an appointment. A friend of his sent me to him."

"He was expecting you?"

"He knew this friend was going to send someone. I'm the someone."

"I see. Well, you'll just have to wait."

"Try ringing him again," I said to Ruth Marr.

"Don't do it, Ruth," Epsworth said quietly. "You've made enough racket up there as it is. Wait about five minutes, and then you may call him again." He turned to me with a stiff little smirk on his face, and said, "I think that will be better, Mr. Lam."

I nodded.

He stood there for several seconds, his left hand resting possessively on the back of Ruth Marr's chair, the fingers drumming lightly against the wood. His eyes studied me. "You have a car?" he asked.

"Yes," I said.

"Parked near here?"

"Right across the street."

"I see," he said.

I said, "Well, I have a call to make to town. I may as well put that through while I'm waiting," and dove into booth 1. I dropped a dime, and gave the operator the number of Bertha Cool's apartment. It was a relief to hear her voice on the line.

"Listen," I said, "something's happened out here, and I'm afraid I'm mixed in it."

"What?" she asked.

"Something serious," I said.

"For Christ's sake, Donald, don't be like that. You're green at the game. You mustn't get excited over trifles. Bertha's had a hard day at the office, and when she goes home and gets her clothes off, she wants to relax. You're young and active, Donald. You do the leg work. You can report to me in the morning, but you mustn't keep disturbing me—"

I said, "I think a lot of cops are going to be out here pretty quick."

"What's happened, Donald?"

"I don't know," I said, "I don't think anyone else does—yet. Gell doesn't answer his phone. He's supposed to be up there."

"He doesn't answer his phone?"

"No. I don't think he's ever going to answer his phone again."

"Where are you now?"

"At the Mountain Crest Apartments."

She said, "Stay there unless someone takes you to the police station. I'm coming out," and I heard the receiver bang.

I walked out of the booth and looked at my watch. Epsworth had moved a few feet away, but was still standing within earshot. I smiled casually at Ruth Marr, and said, "Well, we may as well try Gell again," and vanished into booth 2. I took down the receiver and heard her voice saying swiftly, "He smells a rat. He's called the cops. *Number please? What number? Oh, Mr. Gell's room? Oh, yes, how stupid of me. I'll ring again.*"

There was a long period during which I could hear the sound made by the button which rang the telephone bell and very faintly the sound of a man's voice talking rapidly. I gathered the voice was that of George Epsworth, the night clerk, giving swift instructions to Ruth Marr.

After a moment, she said, "He doesn't answer. Mr. Epsworth thinks it's useless to call him any more now. He says you'd better wait for ten or fifteen minutes."

I said, "Thanks," hung up the telephone, and came out of the booth. Epsworth said, "I think you'd better wait ten or fifteen minutes, Mr. Lam, and then try again. Then if he doesn't answer, I'll go up myself and see if everything's all right."

I said, "Thank you."

"You say you're parked across the street?"

"Yes."

"You'll be waiting over there in your car?"

"Yes."

Ruth looked at me. There was agony in her eyes, but she had no chance to say anything. I crossed the lobby, went out through the door, and over to the agency car. I climbed in and sat down, waiting.

About five minutes later, I saw Ruth come to the door of the apartment house. I saw her silhouetted against the lighted interior, and, directly behind her, the form of Epsworth. He said something, and Ruth half turned, as though to push him away. Epsworth took her arm and pulled her around. As she turned, she waved her hand in a gesture toward me. It was a gesture that meant go away—"beat it."

I ignored it because I had to ignore it. No matter what happened, I had to sit there. Eventually, it was all going to come out, how I'd been hired to shadow Cunner, how Cunner was Gell, how I'd been on the job for Bertha Cool, and how it was my duty to stay there watching the apartment house until twelve-thirty A.M. Otherwise, it would have been running away, and in my position I didn't want to do anything which looked like running away.

I sat there thinking, thinking. Bertha Cool was on her way out. Cops were on their way out. Cunner was dead. I knew where the gun was that had shot him. I was the only one who *did* know. The night clerk had notified the law. He was wise to something. He wanted me to stay right there. He didn't want me to leave.

Twenty minutes passed, minutes which were just a procession of orderly rounds on the second hand of the dash clock on Bertha Cool's new automobile.

A car swung in behind me. Headlights bored through the window in the rear of the car. The driver changed his mind about parking behind me and swung alongside.

They were driving very slowly as they eased on past, almost at a crawl. I got a look at their license number. It was a cop car all right. Both cops got out, the driver on his side, the other man through the right-hand door to the curb. They converged on me.

The cop on my side swung one foot to the running board of

my car, and said, "Okay, buddy, what is it?" He flashed his star.

I looked at him. "A stakeout," I said. "I'm tailing a guy."

The officer on the other side opened the door and slid into the car. "Let's see your driving license, buddy," he said.

"Suppose you boys play ball on your side of the street," I said. "I'm covering mine."

"None of your lip," the officer on the other side said, opening the door. "What about that license, buddy?"

I showed it to them.

"Let's see the rest of it," he said.

"Rest of what?"

"Your license as a private dick."

I passed it out, a certificate showing that I was Donald Lam, a private investigator, working for Bertha Cool.

"Bertha Cool, eh," one of the men said. The other one laughed, and said, "If this runt is a detective, I'm the heavy-weight champion of the world."

The man who had his foot on the running board of the car seemed to be the boss. "Shut up, Carl," he said. "Let's get the straight of this." He turned to me and asked, "What are you doing here, buddy?"

"If you want to know anything about me," I said, "ask the boss. She's in the department that gives out the information."

"Well, you're giving it out right now," the man said ominously. "What are you doing out here?"

"Flying a kite."

The men exchanged glances. "Okay," the leader said, "let's go."

The man on my side wrapped my necktie around his wrist and nearly broke my neck jerking me out of the automobile. They gave me the bum's rush across the street and into the apartment house. The night clerk was waiting for us. Ruth looked up, startled.

"You the guy that put in the call?" the officer asked the night clerk.

Epsworth nodded.

"All right, what's it all about?"

"Man by the name of Gell in six hundred," the night clerk said. "This chap," indicating me, "has been acting queer, hanging around, asking questions about Gell, pumping the janitor, pumping the switchboard operator, and watching the elevators.

"Earlier this evening, this guy comes in and tips off the girl at the switchboard. She makes a stall that she's going to the restroom, but she doesn't go. She goes to the second floor and takes the elevator up to the sixth. I think he was with her. While she was up there, Gell's light flashes on the board. I take down the receiver, and she screams and hangs up. Since she came back, she's been ringing Gell's apartment, and he doesn't answer. Maybe it's all right, but it looks fishy to me."

"Why didn't you go up and investigate?"

"Because I know the minute I did, she'd tip him off and he'd beat it. If there's anything wrong, I wanted you to catch him right on the job."

The officers exchanged glances, then they looked at me.

"The guy's nuts," I said.

"What's your interest in Gell, buddy?"

"Ask Bertha Cool," I said.

The officers turned to size up the night clerk.

"While Miss Marr was supposed to be in the restroom, she went up to that apartment," he said positively.

"Go on up, Carl," the leader said. "Take this guy with you. He'll show you the apartment. Take a look around. I'll keep these two down here."

One of the officers said to Epsworth, "Come on," and entered the elevator. The officer left behind with Ruth and me said,

"Get over to the switchboard, sister. Don't put through any out-going calls unless you tell me about them and let me listen in. Don't call any rooms and don't try to talk with this bird."

Ruth gave me a white-faced glance, then marched back to the switchboard. The officer sized me up with a slow grin twisting the corners of his mouth. "Detective, eh?" he asked.

We stood there silently for what seemed ages. I watched the indicator of the elevator creep slowly up until it came to a stop on the dial opposite six. Then I saw it waver into motion, and come slowly back down the dial until the lighted doorway showed in the lobby, and the officer and the white-faced night clerk came out.

The officers exchanged glances. The man who had been up in the elevator said, "Notify Homicide, Fred. I'll go back and sew the place up. You keep these guys down here. Don't let them talk."

"You're sure?" the officer with me asked.

"Uh huh. A bullet right past his fountain pen. I wouldn't be a hell of a lot surprised if it was fired from the back."

The night clerk said, "I knew that—"

"Shut up," they both chorused, as though they'd rehearsed the act.

Epsworth shut up.

The officer in charge walked over to Ruth Marr, started to say something, then noticed the telephone booth that was a pay station. "That an outside line?" he asked.

She nodded, but couldn't trust her voice. He went into the booth, took down the receiver, and dialed. His broad shoulders concealed the telephone from us. The motions of the back of his head and neck showed that he was talking. He was talking for some little time, then he came out, motioned to the other chap, and said, "Go on and sew the place up."

He turned to us and said, "I don't want any conversation. I don't want anyone to try to give a signal. You folks will have your chance to talk later on. Right now you keep quiet."

I lit a cigarette and avoided Ruth Marr's eyes.

George Epsworth said, "May I talk with you, officer? May I—"

"No," the officer said.

Epsworth adopted a position of injured dignity, but he kept quiet.

After a while, I heard the sound of a siren in the distance. The siren became rapidly louder, and the rays of a red spotlight illuminated the front of the apartment house. The car skidded into the curb and slapped on the brakes. Men came spewing through the door and filled the lobby. For a while, the officer was busy answering questions and the elevators were moving regularly back and forth. Then things quieted down, and I found myself in the custody of a slender chap with keen eyes who started asking me questions.

"I'm on a job," I said. "I have nothing to say about what kind of a job it is. You'll have to ask my boss about that. I was interested in a tenant here in the building. I was shadowing him, and I was getting paid for it."

"All right, who is this tenant?"

I shook my head.

The man's eyes grew hard and thoughtful. "Just asking for it, aren't you?" he said ominously.

Abruptly the swinging door banged open. It seemed for a moment as though it were going to leave its hinges and keep right on going. Then it shivered in protest, and started back. Bertha Cool, who had taken the door right in her stride with a stiff arm that would have done credit to an all-American football player, came flowing into the room.

"Hello," she said.

The officer who had me in charge looked up at her. "What," he asked, "do you want?"

"Not a goddamn thing," Bertha Cool said cheerfully.

I wished the guy off on her. "That," I said, "is the boss."

He looked over at her and said, "Oh."

Bertha Cool pushed her way up in front of him. "What are you doing," she said, "with my operative?"

"Holding him," the officer said.

"All right," Bertha Cool said, "quit holding him. I need him in my business. Ask me what you want to know, and I'll tell you. He won't tell you anything. He isn't paid to talk."

"What's he doing out here?" the officer demanded.

Bertha Cool took a cigarette from her purse. Her eyes flicked to mine. I clamped my lips closely together to let her know that I hadn't said anything. She struck a match, lit the cigarette, and said, "We had a tail job, chap by the name of Cunner, works as an assistant buyer for Webley & McMarr Company. His wife thought he was cheating. He was. He has an apartment here under the name of Gell. He was here last night with a blonde. We shadowed him. That's all there is to it."

"What got you out of bed?" the officer said.

"I wasn't in bed," she said, "and when my operative failed to telephone in his regular report, I figured he was taking a joyride with some tart in the company car. I decided I'd do something about it. Now you tell me what's the trouble."

"I'm not giving out any information," he said.

"Well, the place is certainly lousy with cops," Bertha Cool observed. "Do you know what's happened, Donald?"

The man said to me, "Don't tell her."

I said, "Apparently something's happened to Gell. He didn't answer his telephone, and—"

The officer swung his open hand against my lips, knocking

me back. I could feel the taste of blood where my teeth cut the lip.

"Shut up," he said. "I told you not to talk."

Bertha Cool said, "All right, Donald. Don't talk then. Don't say another goddamn word until *I* tell you to." She looked at the officer, and said, "Try swinging against *my* mouth."

"I will, if you talk out of turn," the officer told her.

Bertha Cool said, "It's the policy of my agency to cooperate, but when you deliberately beat up my operatives when they're trying to give you information, I know what to do about it. See?"

"He wasn't trying to give me information. He was trying to give it to you."

"Oh you think so, do you?"

"I know it."

Bertha Cool puffed contentedly away at her cigarette.

A car drew up outside, and more officers came in, and then, somewhere in the crowd, I saw Mrs. Atterby and Mrs. Cunner bustling forward. Mrs. Atterby was in the lead. "What's happened, Mrs. Cool?" she asked.

Bertha Cool said, "All I know is what I told you, that Eben Cunner has an apartment here under the name of Gell. His sister is supposed to be living with him."

"Who's this?" the officer asked.

Bertha Cool smiled at him and said, "These are my clients."

The officer was impressed. He turned to Mrs. Atterby. "What's your connection with this?" he asked.

"With what?"

"With this."

Mrs. Atterby pushed her jaw out at him. Her eyes snapped. "I don't know what you're referring to," she said, "and I object to being addressed in that tone of voice."

The officer said, "Are you Mrs. Gell?"

"I am not."

He jerked his head toward Mrs. Cunner, who was standing fat and helpless, looking as though she'd make a nosedive if she could find some place for a landing. A handkerchief was clasped in her right hand, halfway to her eyes. "Is *this* Mrs. Gell?" he asked.

Bertha Cool said, "Yes," and Mrs. Atterby said, "No."

The officer remembered something. "How about Cunner?" he asked. "Is this Mrs. Cunner."

"Yes."

He said, "Just a minute. Wait here." Then he stopped one of the officers, and said, "Tell the sergeant I think we have someone who can identify the body."

Mrs. Atterby said, "My poor child," and folded Edith Cunner into her arms.

Bertha Cool smoked placidly.

After a while, a couple of officers came and ushered Mrs. Atterby and Edith Cunner toward the elevator. They went up. Ten minutes later they came down. Mrs. Cunner was having hysterics. Newspaper photographers exploded flash lamps in their faces.

Bertha Cool caught Mrs. Atterby's eye. "How about it?" she asked.

One of the officers said, "No talking, please."

Mrs. Atterby said, "It's Eben. He's been shot—"

The officer got between them and jostled Mrs. Atterby through the door and into an automobile. They were whisked away.

The lobby was jammed full of people. After a while, someone called my name, and an officer piloted me into the elevator, took me to the sixth floor, but didn't take me into Gell's apartment.

Instead he took me down the corridor to where a sergeant was seated at a table. A shorthand stenographer was taking notes. A couple of detectives were standing with their hats on, smoking, and looking wise.

"What's your name?"

"Donald Lam."

"What's your occupation?"

"I'm an operative for the Bertha Cool Detective Agency."

"What were you doing out here?"

"Working."

"Tailing this man, Cunner?"

"I was told not to answer questions."

"Who told you?"

"Bertha Cool."

"Well, we're telling you different."

"One of these officers struck me across the face because I tried to answer questions," I said.

One of the detectives said, "It would be tough if you got another smash because you *didn't* answer questions."

"You get Bertha Cool in here," I said, "and if she tells me to talk, I'll talk."

The sergeant hesitated a minute, and then said to the man at the door, "Okay, bring her in."

A few moments later, Bertha Cool came pushing her way into the room, completely at her ease.

"Now go ahead and talk," the officer told me.

I glanced at Bertha.

"It's all right, Donald," she beamed at me. "Go ahead and tell the *gentlemen* anything they want to know."

I said, "Mrs. Atterby and Mrs. Cunner employed the agency. That was yesterday. I went out last night to pick up Cunner. I picked him up at the place where he worked. I tailed him here.

He had a car staked out at a downtown garage. He picked up a blonde somewhere along the line. The blonde was supposed to be his sister. I never did find out who she was. I lost them last night when my car got rained on and wouldn't start. I picked him up tonight and tagged him here."

I saw Bertha Cool's eyes glint with approval because I held out information about the Orange Cove Apartments.

"What did you do after you got here?" the sergeant asked.

"Waited," I said.

"Just sat in the car and waited?"

"I tried to size up what was doing," I said. "I hung around the switchboard as much as I could, trying to get information about who his visitors were, and I made some inquiries at the garage trying to find out whether his sister was here."

"You didn't go up on the sixth floor tonight?"

"Me?"

"Yes, you. Who the hell do you think we're talking about?"

"No, certainly not. This is the first time I've been up here."

"The night clerk says the girl at the switchboard took a powder, that you joined her, and came up to the sixth floor."

"He's a liar."

The sergeant twisted a lead pencil in his fingers, and said, absently, "I'm not so certain but what he is myself." He turned to Bertha Cool and asked, "What was this, a divorce case?"

"Uh huh."

"How did the women get wise to this place?"

"I notified them."

His eyes narrowed.

"You notified them of what?"

"That Mr. Cunner was out here under the name of Gell, that if they wanted to catch him with the blonde, all they had to do was to come out here and nail him."

"But you didn't know the blonde was here, did you?"

"I figured she would be."

"How long have you been working on the case?"

"This is the second night."

"Why didn't you string it along until you had the stage all set?"

She beamed at him, and said, "I was working on a minimum guarantee."

"Oh," he said.

He turned back to me. "How about this girl at the switch-board?"

"What about her?"

"Friendly with her?"

"I took her home last night."

"Directly home?"

"No, we stopped and had a bite to eat at the Yucca Club."

"Dance?"

"Uh huh."

"Do any petting?"

"What do *you* think?"

"She didn't tell you anything about this man, Gell, did she?"

"Nothing I didn't know already."

"What was the idea?"

"I was pumping her for information."

"That's right," Bertha Cool interpolated. "It's all in his signed report."

The sergeant seemed a little bored. He said, "What we want is to find out about that blonde."

"We do, too," Bertha Cool said.

He looked searchingly at me. "You haven't any idea who she was?"

"No."

"You have a good description of her?"

"Yes."

"And you'd know her if you saw her again?"

"Yes."

"I think that's important," he said. "Don't talk to the newspaper reporters. Give me the description."

"She's twenty-seven," I said, "about five feet one, weight about a hundred and twelve. The last time I saw her she wore a black dress with a short, full skirt that showed her legs to advantage. She had good-looking silver fox furs, big expensive ones, and a small, black hat. She has blue eyes, and rather a round face. She has a trick of tilting her chin up to one side when she laughs, and she has a cooing voice."

"Look like a gold digger?" the sergeant asked.

"Yes."

The sergeant stared at me steadily. "You didn't notice anything else about this man, did you?" he asked. "Didn't find out anything about his visitors—any of the people who came to call on him?"

Bertha Cool interposed, "When a man has a blonde like that in an apartment, he doesn't have visitors. Don't be silly."

The sergeant kept his eyes on me. "I'm asking him," he said.

"I tell you I was only on the job one night," I said. "I—"

"Don't argue with him, Donald," Bertha Cool interposed. "I have copies of your reports here. The sergeant can have them if he wants."

"I want 'em," the sergeant said.

Bertha Cool passed over a typewritten sheet of three paragraphs. The sergeant read down through it thoughtfully. "Hell of a report," he said.

Bertha beamed at him. "Ain't it," she agreed.

He looked across at me, and said, "I don't see any reason for you two being detained. Now listen, the newspaper reporters will want to question you. It's going to interfere with our work if there's too much publicity. Suppose you folks could sneak out by the back entrance and make a getaway?"

I met his eyes. "Is there a back entrance?" I asked.

"Of course there is, the tradesmen's entrance."

"I don't know where it is."

He nodded to one of the detectives. "Show 'em out, Jim," he said. "First frisk this guy."

The man he addressed went to work, searching first for a gun, then going through my pockets. They listed everything they found.

The sergeant jerked his head toward the door. "Take 'em out," he said.

The detective pulled his hat down a half inch on his forehead, said, "This way," and barged toward the door.

As we drove away in the agency car, Bertha Cool said, "Remember, Donald, you're working for Bertha. We deal in information. The stuff you get is only for Bertha. You mustn't give it to anyone else."

"Uh huh," I said.

"And that means the cutie who works at the switchboard," she pointed out.

When I didn't say anything, Bertha Cool heaved one of those tremulous sighs. "Christ," she complained to no one in particular, "he's in love again."

"How did Mrs. Atterby find out about it?" I asked.

Bertha Cool's glance was pitying. "I told them, of course," she said. "Good God, Donald, you didn't want to have them read about it tomorrow in the newspaper, did you? That would be an awful black eye for the agency."

"You mean you told them the man was murdered?"

"Of course not, Donald. I told them that he was out at the

apartment, and that you were on the job out there, that if they wanted to come out and look the setup over and get a look at the blonde, it was all right with me."

"And my reports?" I asked.

"I had to go down to the office and type those up myself," she said. "That's why I was so long getting there. I knew they'd want your reports, and I didn't dare give them the real reports."

"Why?"

Her eyes half closed, seemed to recede into the pouches of fat which surrounded them. "Because," she said, "you're valuable to me, Donald. If I'd submitted the reports that showed you knew who had been calling on Gell—that you could positively identify the officers and the firemen—well, Donald, my love, you'd have been found in an alley somewhere with a lot of bullet holes in you. You remember, Donald, Bertha spoke to you about that once before."

"I remember," I said, "but I don't see just why."

"If you knew who Premmer was," she said, "you'd understand."

"Who," I asked, "is Premmer?"

"Naughty, naughty," she said.

"Oh, all right," I told her. "I can find out without you telling me."

She thought that over for a while, and then said, "He's the big squeeze in the Civil Service Department, Donald, my love. Now keep quiet, and let Bertha think."

Chapter VII.

Bertha Cool took a notebook from her pocket and jotted down the mileage on the agency car when I arrived at her apartment.

"Just to make it businesslike, Donald, my love," she said, "and to keep temptation out of your way."

"Do you want me to leave the bus standing on the street?" I asked.

"No, lover, you can put it in a garage. Bertha will make allowances for that. Bertha is always just with you, Donald, but don't think you can take that switchboard baby and do any joy-riding with the agency car, precious, because you can't get away with it."

"How about keeping this bus in the garage where Gell kept his?"

"How far is that from the office?"

"About six blocks."

"Too far, lover. Find someplace that's closer."

"Looking around will run up the odometer," I said.

She turned to me. "Listen, Donald, I don't know what you're up to, and I don't give a damn, but you'll have exactly five miles leeway. After that, every mile that's on the odometer costs you ten cents, and every week Bertha's going to have a mechanic look at the odometer connections. If they've been discon-nected, you lose your job, lover. Now get the hell out of here. Bertha has a lot of things to figure out."

I checked on the odometer reading, and made time to the garage where Gell kept his car. I drove in and said to the parking attendant, "At least an hour—probably all night."

He gave me a ticket. I slipped it in my pocket and walked out nonchalantly. Five minutes later, after he'd had a chance to park the car, I came back on foot. He was sitting in a customer's car with the radio blaring away full tilt. I waved the ticket at him, said, "Going to get some things out of the glove compartment," and walked toward the back part of the garage.

It took me three or four minutes to locate Gell's car. The attendant hadn't paid any attention to where I was going. He was still up in front playing the radio.

I went through the glove compartment of the Gell car. I found a compact, a pair of woman's pigskin driving gloves, some slip-on dark glasses, and a couple of dozen oblongs of perforated silk. That silk puzzled me. They were black oblongs, about eight inches long by four inches wide, and perforated with two rows of "windows." I noticed they weren't all perforated the same.

It was too much junk to carry around in my pocket, so I crossed over and put the whole schmear in the glove compartment of the agency automobile. Then I went back and did some more investigating on the Gell car. There were still bits of mud imbedded in the nonskid marks on the tops of the tires. I figured the bus hadn't been used since the rain of the night before. It had been raining when Cunner had put it in the garage. When the attendant had parked it, the mud and clay in the tire were still wet. It had dried out during the day. Any driving would have caused the dirt to drop off onto the road.

I couldn't afford to use the agency car at ten cents a mile. I walked out and took a streetcar, giving the garage attendant the high sign on the way out.

It was around eleven when I took stock of the situation at the tradesmen's entrance of the Orange Cove Apartments. The door was locked, but the lock was made so the key of any tenant would fit it, and it didn't take much exploring to find a key that would do the work.

I walked into the back hallway. It was stuffy and smelly. Transoms were open for ventilation. I could hear a man snoring regularly. From behind another transom, I heard a giggle and a girl's voice saying, "Don't do *that*." I didn't pay any attention to the sounds, but found the back stairs and tiptoed up. I knew that 208 would be near the end of the corridor, but didn't know whether it would be the back end or the front end.

It was the back end. The door was locked. It wasn't much of a lock, but a lock just the same. I moved quietly out to the service porch to take a look around and saw a window that I figured would be over the sink in the kitchenette. It was a half window just like the one in the apartment I'd looked at—the one that the sun was supposed to come "pouring through in the morning."

I slipped off my shoes and tied the laces together. I hung them around my neck, tested a garbage pail to make certain it was strong enough, and climbed up. I raised the sash and slid my legs through.

I groped for the kitchen sink with my stockinged feet, found it, squeezed in through the opening, and did a turn when I was halfway through the window so that I didn't break my back. I let myself down on the floor of the apartment, put on my shoes, and walked on into the other room. I had a pocket flashlight and switched it on.

It was a crummy joint, just about like the one I'd looked at downstairs. The place was ancient, and needed to be done over. The wallpaper was grimy. The carpet was thin and faded. The upholstery on the chairs was shiny with age. The furniture had been given a new coat of varnish. It hadn't done a hell of a lot of good.

A whiskey bottle and two empty glasses were on the table in the combined sitting and bedroom. The place stunk with the smell of a cold cigar. I located the half-smoked butt on one of the trays. Another held two cigarettes which had been ground out after less than an inch had been smoked. There were also half a dozen cigarette stubs. I turned them over carefully with my finger, looking for lipstick. I couldn't find any.

The whiskey glasses were sticky. Two glasses of water for chasers hadn't been touched. I tried to figure that. Two men had gone up to that apartment just before Cunner had left. Two visitors and Cunner should have meant three glasses. There were only two. Cunner, then, hadn't bought these two cops a drink. The glasses were left over from the visit of the lone speed cop.

I scouted around looking for a telephone. I found it, and, figuring the number would be unlisted, took my notebook from my pocket, pulled out a pencil, and had just finished jotting down the number when the light switch clicked, and a man's voice said, "I thought so."

I whirled around.

Two men stood in the doorway. They'd let themselves in so quietly I hadn't heard the sound of the key in the lock. One of the men still had his finger on the light switch. The other was holding a very businesslike gun.

"Oh, hello," I said casually.

The shorter man kicked the door shut. "Stick 'em up," he said.

I put the pencil back in my pocket, closed my notebook, and dropped it in my inside coat pocket.

The man came forward, jabbing the gun at me with nervous gestures. "I said, 'Stick 'em up,'" he ordered.

The big man who was standing by the light switch watched

me with narrowed eyes. "Take it easy, Alfred," he said. "We don't want any shooting. He isn't going to try to pull a gun now."

"The hell he isn't," Alfred said. "You can't tell about these little bastards. They're nervous and they have more guts than the big guys."

I said quietly, "Why would I want to pull a gun?" and walked toward the door.

"Nuts," the guy with the gun said.

The big man moved slowly around to meet me, his arms swinging loosely from his shoulders like a prizefighter walking toward the center of the ring, ready to lash out with either hand. He was in the early forties and was over six feet tall. He wore a neatly pressed, pearl gray suit, tan shoes, a striped silk shirt, and a tie of gray with fine red stripes running down it.

I heard motion behind me. The big man said, "Not with the gun, Al."

I whirled and flung up my arm to protect my head against the gun barrel. The big man's fist, crashing through under my upraised arm, caught me on the point of the jaw. I felt my heels dragging along the floor as I jerked backward, crashed into a chair, and lost interest in everything.

I came to as the big man was picking me up. He was keeping up a running fire of conversation. I was too groggy to understand all the words. They flowed through my consciousness in a steady stream of sound—sound that was, for the most part, without significance. "—unconscious—can't talk—got to find out—how the hell he knew—can't go through with this thing unless we know what we're up against—playing with dynamite and haven't sense enough to know—he's coming around now. How do you feel, buddy?"

I wiggled my jaw to make certain that it wasn't broken. The

big man said, "Right down here in this chair," and slammed me down in the overstuffed chair. He jerked my hands up, and Al held them by the wrists. The big man went through my pockets, pulling out everything I had, going over each article carefully before he put it back. Then he said, "Let him go, Al. He hasn't a gun. He's harmless as a fly."

Alfred let go my wrists. The big man stepped back and looked at me appraisingly. Alfred said suddenly, "Someone coming, Ralph."

The big man, moving with alacrity, stepped toward the light switch. "You hold him, Al," he said, and clicked out the lights.

Alfred's fingers gripped the collar of my coat.

I could hear boards creaking rhythmically as someone walked steadily down the corridor. There was no sound of footfalls, just the creaking of boards as though a heavy safe was being rolled along on rubber-tired wheels.

I knew the answer even before I heard the surreptitious turning of the doorknob. I started to say something, then decided we might as well make the party complete.

The door opened and closed. I could hear the rustle of motion, the sound of heavy breathing. The light switch clicked on. Bertha Cool stood just inside the doorway, blinking her eyes to accustom them to the light. I was hoping she'd have a gun in her hand, but she didn't. Apparently, she was taken completely by surprise, but nothing in her face showed it. She said, "Hello, everybody," and walked calmly over to the davenport and sat down.

The creaky davenport groaned in protest. I thought the legs were going to give way. It managed to stand the strain, although the high-pitched *ping-g-g-g* from the depths of the cushions indicated that a spring had given up the ghost.

Bertha Cool opened the bag she was carrying in her hand. I

noticed automatically that the diamonds were all gone from her fingers—evidently Bertha was willing to take chances with her body, but not with her diamonds.

Alfred yelled, "Look out, she has a gun in that bag!" The big man, peering over her shoulders, ready to grab her arm if necessary, relaxed as Bertha Cool took out a cigarette case, extracted a cigarette, and said, "How about a light, good-looking?"

He laughed then, snapped a match into flame, leaned forward, and gave Bertha Cool a light.

"Well," she said. "We all seem to be here." She looked across at me, and her eyes grew hard. "I didn't think it of you, Donald," she said.

I didn't say anything. The big man said, "Don't blame him. We're holding him here against his will."

Bertha said, "He should be home in bed."

The tall man said, "You'll pardon me if we go through your purse. We want to find who you are and what you're doing."

"I'm Bertha Cool," she said, "head of the B. Cool Detective Agency."

"Oh, you're the one this guy's working for," the man said, indicating me with a jerk of the head.

"He was," Bertha Cool said. "He's fired now."

"I'll just take a look anyway," the man told her, and took Bertha Cool's purse from her unresisting fingers. Alfred watched him anxiously while he went through everything in the purse. When he was finished, he handed it back to her and looked significantly at Alfred. Then he turned to me and said, "How long were you here before we showed up?"

"About a minute," I said.

"What did you find?"

"You searched me," I told him.

The big man said, "You watch them, Al. Don't let them talk, and don't let them make any moves. Be careful they don't make any jumps toward the telephone. I'm going to frisk the place."

He made a methodical search, going through every nook and corner of the apartment. I sat silent. Bertha Cool smoked calmly. As nearly as I could judge, the big man found nothing. When he had finished, he said, "All right, Al, we scram."

"How about these two?" Alfred asked.

"We leave them here.—Listen, you two, we're going to give you a break. We're going to leave you here. We're not going to get rough about it, but if you try to leave within the next ten minutes, you're going to run into a *lot* of hard luck. Do you understand?"

Bertha Cool said, "Nuts."

Alfred said, "The little guy knows something. He knows something he held out on the agency. That's what she meant by saying he was fired. How the hell did he know about this joint in the first place?"

The big man crossed over to stand in front of me. He raised his left hand to the back of his head, scratched his scalp, and frowned down at me. "Damned if I don't believe Al is right," he said.

I said nothing.

Suddenly he reached down, grabbed the knot of my necktie, jerked me to my feet, and said, "How about it, runt?"

I made a swing for his jaw, but he tightened his hand on my necktie, and choked off my wind. I kicked at him, and he slammed the heel of his hand into my face, jerking my head back until I thought it was going to break my neck.

Bertha Cool, watching us with calm impassivity, blew smoke through her wide nostrils, and said to the big man, "I wouldn't do that if I were you. He's poison."

The big man let go of my tie and I stumbled backwards, felt the chair behind me, and sat down. He said, "The goddamn little runt. He kicked my shin." He swung his left hand and then his right against my jaw in swift slaps. I came up out of the chair swinging with everything I had. Behind me I sensed motion from Alfred. Bertha Cool said, "Look out, lover." I jerked my head to one side to see the gun barrel glittering over my head. I tried to duck—and all the lights went out. It felt as though the roof of the building had caved in on my head.

It seemed like hours later a white-hot gimlet was boring into my brain. I tried to get away from it and couldn't. Then gradually my eyes focused on the incandescent bulb of an electric light which was making torture for my wounded head. I managed to move my head so the light wasn't glaring into my eyes, made tasting noises with my mouth, and tried to get to my feet. My knees buckled, and I went down. I tried to twist my head around to see where I was. The motion nauseated me. I heard Bertha Cool's voice seeming to come from a long ways off saying, "It's all right, lover. They're gone." Her hands slid under my shoulders.

I made another try, and this time, with a lift from Bertha, got into the chair. I felt the back of my head. There was blood on my hand. Bertha Cool took a deep drag of cigarette smoke, exhaled through her distended nostrils, and asked, smokily, "Can you listen to talk, Donald?"

"I guess so," I said wearily.

She said, "I thought better of you, Donald. Bertha wanted to cut herself a piece of cake, and you had to jump in and try to scrape off the frosting."

"How long ago did they leave?" I asked.

"Three or four minutes," she said. "You weren't unconscious long, lover."

"We've got to get out of here," I told her. "Don't you see? They'll notify the cops."

"Why the cops?" she asked.

"Because," I said, "they want a fall guy for that murder."

It hurt me to talk. It hurt me to think. My head was throbbing, but I knew what had to be done. Bertha Cool took another drag at her cigarette and said, "You may be right, Donald. There's nothing left for us here. Come on, lover."

I lurched to my feet, looked around, and found my hat. When I tried to put it on my head, it irritated my scalp wound. So I crumpled it and held it under my arm.

Bertha Cool was big, but her muscles were big enough and powerful enough to move her body easily. She got up from the davenport as smoothly as though she'd been a slim-waisted dancer. "All right, lover," she said, "we'll talk it over outside."

"Better take the back stairs," I suggested.

"No, Donald," she said. "The back stairs look furtive. Come right down the front stairs with Bertha. Better switch out the lights, Donald. Wipe things off with your handkerchief—the doorknob, and the whiskey bottle if you've touched that. I wouldn't leave fingerprints if I were you."

I switched out the lights. We walked together down the corridor. A party was going on somewhere in the front of the house with women laughing in that shrill-voiced, uncontrollable hysteria which comes from too much liquor.

Bertha Cool moved on toward the open air, majestically as a big liner plowing out toward the sea. When we reached the sidewalk, she turned to the left, tucked her arm through mine, and said, "So you chiseled on me, you little bastard."

"What do you mean?" I asked.

"You know what I mean, Donald. You knew Bertha was trying to cut herself a piece of cake. You thought you'd get in on the ground floor and sell Bertha out."

"Bunk," I said. "I knew they were going to try and frame the murder on Ruth Marr, and I intended to stop them."

She missed a step while she thought that over, then she laughed, and said, "Donald, lover, you're just damn fool enough to do that very thing. I believe you're telling the truth."

"Of course, I'm telling the truth," I said. "What the hell did you *think* I went there for?"

She gave me a sidelong glance, and said, "Let's turn down to this other boulevard, Donald, darling. You may be able to get me a taxi.—You didn't come in the agency car?"

"Not at ten cents a mile," I said. "I could walk cheaper than that."

She chuckled, and then said abruptly, "Donald, you were messing around that Gell car, weren't you?"

"I looked it over," I said.

"What did you find?"

"Not much of anything. Some gloves and some pieces of silk."

"Pieces of silk, Donald?"

"Yes."

"What kind of silk, lover?"

"Black silk oblongs with parallel rows of perforations in them."

"All the same?" she asked.

"No. They weren't all the same. I didn't think they were all different either, probably three or four different patterns, and—"

I could feel her fingers grip my arm until it seemed as though she was crushing the flesh against the bone. "Where are they now, Donald? What did you do with them?"

"I put them in a safe place," I said.

She took a deep breath. "Donald, you little bastard, are you trying to hold out on me?"

"I want to know where I stand," I said.

She said, "Donald, darling, you don't have to ask that. You know where you stand with Bertha. Bertha's for you. Bertha's always been for you. She picked you up when you were down and out, Donald, and gave you a job. You don't know much about the business, but Bertha is teaching it to you."

"I'll say you are!" I said bitterly. "What was this about being fired?"

"That was because I thought you'd been trying to chisel on me, lover. It's all right now. Where are those pieces of silk?"

"Look here," I said. "Let's be fair about this. They're going to try and pin that kill on Ruth Marr. I know they are. I'm going to protect her."

"Has she any money, Donald?"

"I don't know. I don't think so."

"If she doesn't employ the agency to protect her interests, lover, you can't do anything except in your spare time."

"I'm not talking about time," I said. "I'm just warning you that I'm going to protect her."

"Do anything you want to, lover—on your own time."

"All right," I said. "I just want that understood. There's not going to be any argument about that."

"Not if you don't do it on agency time, lover."

"All right," I said. "The pieces of silk are in the glove compartment of the agency car."

Bertha Cool stepped in under a streetlight and touched my scalp with tender fingers. "Poor boy," she said. "He's always getting beaten up. That's a nasty wound. You'd better come up to the apartment with me, Donald, and let me wash it out with antiseptic.—I think this is a taxi coming, lover. Hold up your arm and flag him down."

Chapter VIII.

The door to Bertha Cool's private office was closed when I reported for duty. Elsie Brand stopped her typing long enough to say, "Beat it. Bertha says she doesn't want you anywhere around the office this morning. You're not to be where anyone can see you and—"

She broke off as the door of Bertha Cool's private office opened explosively, and a man came barging out, looking as though he was in a hurry to get to the open air.

I flashed him a quick look and saw it was one of the firemen whom I'd seen go to Gell's apartment at Yucca City, one of the men who had said Premmer sent him.

I half turned my back, trying to make myself seem inconspicuous, but his eye caught my face. I saw him jerk his head half around to look me over. Then he crossed the office and was gone.

Bertha Cool came from behind her desk to stand in the doorway of her private office, blotting out the light from the window behind her. "That was unfortunate, lover," she said.

"Wasn't it?" I said. "Why didn't you tip me off he was going to be here?"

"I didn't know it. I told Elsie to get rid of you as soon as you came in."

"Well," I said, "he knows who was on the job now."

She said, "Oh well, it won't hurt anything, lover. He thinks I have half a dozen different operatives; that we'd been working on Gell for a month."

"You mean, that's what you hope he thinks," I said.

She said, "Now, don't be like that, Donald. Bertha has a living to make."

Elsie Brand, who had stopped typing for a few moments to listen, resumed her hammering of the keyboard. "Come in, Donald," Bertha Cool invited.

I followed her into the office. The place was filled with the disagreeable auric emanations of combating animals, but Bertha Cool seemed calmly placid. "Of course, Donald," she said, "they won't dare to do anything rash. They don't know how much we know. You can trust Bertha for that.—How's your head, lover?"

"Not so bad," I said.

"It did quite a bit of bleeding, but it wasn't a bad cut," she said. "You certainly are thin-skinned, Donald."

I didn't say anything.

She said, "You know, Donald, it would be a nice break for Bertha if we could find this blonde. I think Mrs. Atterby would like that, and you know we still have a couple of days we could use on that case without losing any money."

I still didn't say anything.

"Well, Donald, I didn't want to frighten you. I hoped I could soft-soap it over, but you're too goddamned smart. Do you think he recognized you?"

"I know he did."

"How are you fixed for ready cash, lover?"

"I have plenty."

"What do you mean by plenty?"

"Six or seven dollars."

Bertha Cool made noises with her tongue against the roof of her mouth. She said, "That's not enough money, Donald. You should have plenty in your pocket." She opened a drawer in her desk, took out a cash box, and the morning sunlight, reflecting from the diamonds on her fingers, sent coruscating beams of brilliance radiating about the office as she unlocked the box and handed me a sheaf of twenty-dollar bills.

I stared at it. Then I counted. There were five hundred bucks in twenty-dollar bills in that package.

"What's the idea?" I asked.

"Expense money," she said. "Bertha always sticks by the ones who stick by her. Take the agency car, lover, and, for Christ's sake, keep under cover. Telephone the office once or twice a day. Say that you're Mr. Smith of Portland, Oregon trying to get an appointment with Mr. Lam. If Elsie tells you that Mr. Lam hasn't showed up, you'll know that I don't want you to come around the office, or let anyone know where you are. If she says she thinks Mr. Lam will be in later that day, that means you're to call again in about ten minutes and ask if there's any message for Mr. Smith."

"Why all the precautions?" I asked.

"The telephone line would be tapped," she said casually. "We're dealing with a ring of crooked cops, you know."

"Look here," I demanded, "just how far did you go with that fireman?"

Bertha said, "Now, Donald, don't be like that.—And if Cunner took that Gell car out to the Mountain Crest Apartments, who took it back to the garage where it was stored?"

I felt her eyes boring steadily into mine.

"Donald, you little bastard," she said, "you lost him and faked your report. Come now, Donald, be honest with Bertha. You lost him, didn't you?"

"Only for about half an hour," I said, "just long enough for him to have driven from the Orange Cove Apartments out there to Yucca City."

"How did it happen?" she asked.

I told her.

Bertha Cool stared steadily at me. "I told you not to do that,

Donald," she said. "Operatives always try doing that when they've lost a trail—particularly if they think they can pick it up again.—I thought that was what happened. You haven't learned to lie very well, Donald. Your voice didn't sound right over the telephone when I asked you about the Gell car, and then you changed the subject when I asked you about how he'd made the change. All right, Donald, you're on your own now. Go find that blonde, and don't bother Bertha until you've found her. Just telephone in to Elsie, and remember you're Mr. Smith of Portland, Oregon calling for Mr. Lam, and if you find the blonde, Donald, just say that you'll leave a message for Mr. Lam, that Mr. Smith's wife is with him and is very anxious to see Mr. Lam.—Do you understand that, lover?"

I nodded and said, "Here's something I want you to do. It's important. Trace the numbers of this gun and let me know the answer." I handed her the slip of paper on which I'd written the numbers of the gun Ruth Marr had given me.

Bertha Cool didn't look at the paper. She reached for it mechanically. Her eyes were fastened on me. "Donald," she asked, "is that the number of the murder gun?"

"I don't know."

"Donald, don't hold out on Bertha."

"Can you," I asked, "trace the gun?"

"Yes, lover."

"That's all I want."

Bertha Cool sighed. "You're an obstinate little bastard, Donald. Take good care of that agency car, and don't hang around that Marr girl, Donald. If anyone wanted to pick you up, that's the first place they'd look, and Bertha wouldn't want to have you found in a gutter with a lot of bullet holes in you."

I said, "Look here. Suppose you be frank with me. At least, you owe me that much."

"What do you want, Donald?"

"Have you seen Premmer?"

"Yes."

"What did he say?"

She said, "Premmer's either the best damn liar I've ever seen, or he doesn't know anything about it. He called the police and told them I was trying to blackmail him."

"Were you?"

"Not exactly. Bertha was trying to cut herself a piece of cake, and—"

"And what?" I asked.

"And the knife slipped," she said.

"But I suppose it's *my* finger that'll be cut," I said.

"For Christ's sake, Donald, don't be such a pansy! In this game you'll be getting in jams all the time. Get the hell out of here and lie low until I can find out what it's all about. Bertha won't be idle, lover. Right now I've got something by the tail, and I don't know whether it's a bear, a lion, or just a bunch of bull."

I pulled my hat down low on my forehead, and walked out of the office. Elsie Brand didn't even look up from her typing. Bertha Cool stood in the doorway of her private office, watching me out through the outer door. "Goodbye, lover," she said.

I slammed the door.

I went to the garage first, and got the agency car. The stuff I'd put in the glove compartment had been removed. I wished I'd thought to ask Bertha if she'd taken it, but there was no time for that now. I drove half a dozen blocks and called Ruth Marr's apartment. I was relieved to hear her voice at the other end of the line.

"Donald talking," I said. "How's tricks?"

"So-so."

"Did they give you the works, Ruth?"

"Well, they didn't exactly beat me up with a rubber hose, but they did everything else."

"Are they keeping you under surveillance?"

"Why, I don't know."

"What do you think?"

"Why, Donald, it's never occurred to me. Why should they?"

I said, "Never mind that. This is important. Wait exactly twenty-five minutes, then leave your apartment and start walking down the hill. Turn toward the Yucca Club, and walk slowly. When I drive alongside, hop in the car, and don't waste a lot of words. I have something I want to tell you. Got it?"

"Yes, Donald.—Are we going to take a drive?"

"Uh huh. Just hop in the car and make it snappy."

"You'll have me back in time for work?"

"You won't have to worry about that."

"Okay. Be seeing you," she said, and hung up.

I drove out to Yucca City, keeping my eyes pretty well glued to the minute hand of my three-dollar wristwatch. Ruth Marr was on time to the second. I slid the car in at the curb alongside of her, and said, "Make it snappy, Ruth."

She came in with a quick flash of legs. I gunned the car into motion, and the forward jerk of the machine slammed the door shut. I kept my eyes on the rearview mirror. In it, I saw a woman who had been strolling along the street suddenly raise her arm and wave a white handkerchief. A car shot out to swing into the curb. It stopped long enough to pick her up.

That was all I wanted to know.

Bertha Cool's car did its stuff. There was a service road which went down past the Yucca Grove to a lower entrance, where food was taken in and garbage taken out. That road swung around back to come up on the other side of the parking station. The driver who was following us evidently knew all about that, but didn't know there was a rutted old road which turned off and went directly down the sidehill through the chaparral and manzanita until it hit a boulevard which ran along the canyon.

Ruth gave a little scream when I turned down the steep sidehill road. "Hang on," I told her.

That road had been made back in the days of the Model T Ford when cars had narrow tires and high clearance. I had to straddle the road in several places to get through. I got through. I did a lot of juggling with the steering wheel. I was too busy to listen to Ruth. Nothing came along from behind. The follow car was evidently waiting up at the other end of the service road.

When we hit the boulevard, she said, "Donald, you're the most *won*derful driver—and the most reckless. *Why* did you come down there?"

"Just to see what the car would do," I said, gunning it into speed.

"What did you want to see me about?"

"Lots of things," I told her, "among others, they're going to try and pin that kill on you, and I thought you should know."

"Donald!"

"I'm just telling you," I said.

"Donald, that isn't the truth! It can't be! I told them that I went to the restroom, that I felt badly, had a sudden headache, and—well, you know, felt like the devil. I said I was there ten or fifteen minutes, and that was all I knew. They asked me a lot of questions about Gell's telephone calls and about the blonde, but as far as the others were concerned, they just took it for granted I was telling the truth."

"You just think they did," I said. "Anyhow, that was last night. Today, it's different."

"Why, Donald? What's happened today?"

"Bertha Cool," I said, "tried to cut herself a piece of cake, and the knife slipped. A whole lot of people we don't know anything about are getting busy on us right now."

"What do you mean? What are we going to do?"

I slowed the car so I could look at her. "You and I," I said, "are going to be fugitives from justice until we can find out who killed Arthur Gell."

"You mean I'm not to go to work and—"

"Not going to work," I said, "going to live under an assumed name, and going to be in hiding."

She thought that over for a minute, then said, "With you, Donald, or by myself?"

"By yourself," I said.

Her hand closed over mine. "I'll do what you say, honey—but I'd like to have you—near me—*Please*, Donald!—Just near enough so I can call you—see you."

Chapter IX.

You can never tell about a reformer. Sometimes he's a reformer. Sometimes he's just a politician in a borrowed suit of clothes. I wished I'd known a little more about Judge Carter Longan. The fact that both newspapers poked a little fun at him and treated him as something of a joke made me think he might be on the square. I'd heard him talk twice on the radio. He was the chairman of the Citizens' League of Decency in Civic Government.

His secretary was one of those string bean women who look fifty from the time they're thirty-five until they're past seventy. She looked at me with alert, appraising eyes, and asked for my name.

"Donald Lam," I said. "The business is personal, urgent, and confidential. If I can't see the judge within ten minutes, I don't see him at all."

She looked me over, memorizing every detail of my features so she could give the judge an accurate description. Then she said, "Just a minute," and vanished through the door of the private office.

Judge Longan himself came out when the door opened the second time. He was a big-framed man, stoop-shouldered, somewhere in the early sixties with a great shock of white hair. His lips were thick, but the actual line of his mouth when his lips came together was a straight gash right across his face. His eyes smoldered with an inner fire that his face didn't show. They made an appraisal. He said, in a kindly voice, "Come in, Mr. Lam."

I followed him into his private office. He motioned to his secretary. She went out.

When he looked across at me and raised his busy eyebrows, I said, "My name's Lam. I'm a private detective. I was working for Bertha Cool. I had a shadow job on a man by the name of Cunner. I found he was keeping a blonde in an apartment. He went under the name of Gell—"

"Just a moment," he interrupted. "You're referring to the man who was murdered last night?"

I nodded.

"Go ahead," he said.

"I found that Gell had lots of money," I said. "He had quite a few visitors. They were all men who might have been taking Civil Service examinations. I have the license numbers of the cars in which some half-dozen of his visitors arrived, and descriptions of those visitors. Does that mean anything to you?"

His eyes bored steadily into mine. "I think it does," he said.

I took a sheet of typewritten data from my pocket. "Here it is," I said.

He looked it over. "What," he said, "do you want?"

I waited until his eyes looked up from the typewritten sheet to mine. "Bertha Cool," I said, "played it wrong. She tipped her hand. They're going to try and frame the murder on a girl named Ruth Marr, and on me. I'd like a square deal for both of us. I think you can see that we get it."

He thought that over for almost a minute. "Did you kill him?" he asked conversationally.

"No."

"Do you know who did?"

I said, "It rests between a man named Epsworth, who's night clerk at the Mountain Crest Apartments in Yucca City, whom I don't like, and a mysterious individual, wearing an overcoat and a plaid suit, who entered the apartment house while the girl at the telephone desk was in the restroom."

"Yes," he said, "I read about that person in the paper. The night clerk didn't seem to attach much importance to him."

I said, "That's right. He didn't."

"This typewritten sheet seems to list all the information you have in which I'd be interested."

"That was what I tried to do."

"It doesn't leave you in much of a position to drive a bargain," he said.

"A typewritten sheet can't testify before a grand jury," I said.

"No," he admitted, "I suppose it can't."

"Neither," I said significantly, "can a corpse."

"Suppose," Judge Longan said, after a silence, while he thought that over, "you begin at the beginning and tell me everything you know about the case."

I gave him the highlights. I didn't tell him anything about the gun episode with Ruth Marr, but I gave him most of the facts. When I had finished, Judge Longan said, "You're putting me in a peculiar position, Lam."

"Yes, sir."

He picked up the typewritten report again and studied it carefully. Abruptly he looked at me over the tops of his glasses. "Do you," he asked, "know Ralph Corfitone?"

"I've read of him in the papers and seen pictures, I suppose," I said, "but I don't know him personally."

"Would you know him if you saw him?"

I shook my head.

The judge returned to a study of the report. "You say that Mrs. Cool has been in touch with at least one of the men whom you list as a caller on this man Gell?"

"Yes."

"Do you know what she accomplished?"

"I don't think she accomplished anything," I said, and then added, "As she expressed it, she was trying to cut herself a piece of cake and the knife slipped."

I saw the judge's face relax—not a smile, just a release of the tension on the facial muscles. Then he was once more cold, formidable, and businesslike. "I don't know the object of your visit, Lam," he said, "but I want you to understand that I am *not* going to be placed in the position of standing between you and the law."

"All right," I said.

"I appreciate the information that you have given me."

I got to my feet, and picked up my hat.

He sat looking at me for a moment as though he wanted to say something else but didn't know just how to start in. "What," he asked, "happened to these perforated sheets of silk?"

"I don't know. I put them in the glove compartment of Bertha Cool's car. They're not there now."

"I suppose," he said, "you know what those were."

"No, sir."

"In some of the less important Civil Service examinations," he went on to explain, "where there are large numbers of entrants, the questions are prepared on printed sheets of paper. The left-hand column contains squares to be checked when the answers are negative, and the right-hand, similar squares when the answers are affirmative. The questions are trick questions. That is, they assume, in many instances, certain things which are not true. The person taking the examination is called on to watch tricks of phraseology and check incorrect premises. The questions are all answered 'yes' or 'no.' In grading such examination papers, a sheet of silk is given to the person who marks or grades the papers. That sheet has perforations which are so designed that only the incorrect answers will appear when the sheet is covered by this oblong of silk. In that way, the papers can be graded rather rapidly."

He paused impressively, then said, "You will, of course, realize what would happen if the person taking the examination were furnished in advance with the proper bit of silk. It would only be necessary to surreptitiously cover the sheet of questions to get a perfect score—and without the applicant even having to read the questions."

I said, without interest, "Well, if there's nothing you care to do, I'm sorry I took up your time. I thought that if you knew the true facts, it might help. I know what's going to happen to me. I've tangled with a political machine which has been sopping up the gravy. They want me out of the way. By putting me on the spot for the murder rap, they kill two birds with one stone. After that, anything I say becomes a squawk designed to draw a red herring across the path."

"I appreciate that," he said gravely.

"So do I," I told him.

I was halfway through the door when he said, "I can assure you of one thing, Lam. I'll follow the developments in this case with the greatest interest, and if you should uncover any lead connecting Ralph—" He broke off, shrugged his shoulders, and said, "Perhaps it will be better if I don't go into details. I thank you for coming to me."

I'd hoped he'd see the importance of keeping me alive and as a witness. Evidently, he couldn't. He was willing to use any information I could give him, but wasn't prepared to go to the bat. That was all I wanted to know. It meant his case wasn't ready for the grand jury. I went back to the parking station where I'd left the car with Ruth Marr sitting in it, surrendered my pasteboard ticket to the parking station attendant, climbed in, and started the motor.

I hadn't told Ruth where I was going or what I was going to try to do, so I didn't have any explanations to make.

"Well, kid," I said, "we're on our own."

"Donald, I don't like it."

I laughed, and said, "No one expected you would. Next time, don't go around picking up guns, calling on your man friends, and failing to report to the police when you find dead bodies—"

"Oh, Donald, *don't!*"

I devoted my attention to driving the car.

"Donald," she said after a while, in a thin, pleading voice.

"What?"

"I don't like living by myself. It would be a *lot* better if you were close enough so I could talk to you."

"Talk," I said, "is dangerous."

"Where are you taking me?"

"How good an actress are you?"

"I don't know," she said.

"Could you talk with a foreign accent?"

"What accent?"

"Any kind of an accent," I said, "the goofier the better. Do it mostly with your eyes and hands. You'll be a refugee from one of the European countries, and you don't want to talk about it. You understand only a few words of English. I'll be a clerk from the American Express Company. I'm calling on you, because I'm bringing you mail, and taking care of financial transactions for you. I'm trying to find a congenial, feminine companion of your own race. You're suspicious of all others. You don't know enough English to travel by yourself, and you won't trust any American."

"Why all *that* build-up?" she asked.

"Because," I said, "people are curious. They're always curious about good-looking girls. Lack of information makes for curiosity. Lots of information makes only for interest. Let's give out lots of information. You won't answer any questions. I'll do all the talking. I know a place that specializes in steamship stickers, hotel placards, and things of that sort. Mostly, they sell them for lampshades. I'm going to buy you some secondhand baggage. You can pick up what things you need. We'll paste on the labels, rub dirt over them, scratch off a corner here and there and make you convincing."

If she had any ideas about it, she kept them to herself. I figured we had not more than two hours at the most within which to work. After that, the hue and cry would catch up with us unless we had some tag the public would take for granted.

Three o'clock in the afternoon found us ensconced in a second-rate apartment hotel. Ruth Marr was Yvonne Delmaire. I was Carl Benn of the American Express Company, and I had cards to prove it. She was in 604. I was in 207. The manager was curious, and I took twenty minutes satisfying his curiosity, building up such a colorful background that I almost believed the yarn myself.

The evening newspapers broke the case wide open. A witness had been found who had seen Ruth Marr in the Mountain Crest Apartment House, sneaking down the staircase, carrying a gun, partially concealed by the folds of her skirt. The night clerk had "remembered" more about a mysterious telephone call which had come from the Gell apartment. A light had flashed on the switchboard during the absence of Ruth Marr. He had plugged in a line. Just as he had started to say, "Number please," he had heard a woman's voice scream, "Oh," and he thought she had said, "Donald." Then the phone had been dropped into place.

There was quite a bit more. It was plenty. It might have surprised some of the boys if they could have realized how close to the truth they'd come at that.

It made a nice newspaper story: Donald Lam, the private detective, who was evidently working under an alias, and whose past was veiled in questionable obscurity; Ruth Marr, the telephone operator who had been led on by Gell until she had fallen head-over-heels in love with him, fascinated by his lavish generosity, his free and easy life, driven to an insane jealousy by the "sister" who had entered his life.

I let Ruth read the papers. I thought it would be good for her to know what we were up against.

"Donald," she said, "I got you into this, didn't I?"

"Donald, hell," I said. "I'm Carl Benn, and don't talk without your accent."

She rolled her eyes. "But, Monsieur, it is so—what you call—such a puzzlement—yes—no."

"Better," I said. "You never can tell who's listening outside the transom. You're damn right it's a puzzlement."

"And Yvonne is so much of a frightened."

"Yvonne does well to be frightened," I said. "It's a strange country. You don't know the language very well, and you don't know the customs at all. It's a hard country, and a cruel country, and the only way to get by is to outsmart them."

She showed her dimples as she smiled. "Monsieur is so kind. It is so good of this—what you call—American Express."

"That's right," I said. "You're doing swell, kid. Try saying Express."

I thought the make-believe would perfect her in her part and keep her mind occupied, but she suddenly came across to me as though she'd been tossed in a trapeze act. She flung her arms around my neck, buried her cheek against my coat lapel, and snuggled up in my lap. "Oh, Donald," she said, "I'm responsible for this. I got you into it. If it hadn't been for that damn g-g-gun, I—"

I gave her a smart slap where it would do the most good. "Shut up, Yvonne," I said. "Forget it."

She raised eyes that were glistening with tears. Her mouth showed sudden determination. "Don," she said, "I have to confess something to you."

"Don't," I told her. "Confessing is bad business."

"Donald, no, I have to. You have to know."

"What?" I asked.

"Donald," she wailed tearfully, "I'm a-a-a nymphomaniac."

For a minute, I thought she was kidding, and was debating whether a good spanking would hinder or retard the situation, then I saw she was in tearful earnest.

"Nuts," I said. "You don't even know what you're talking about."

"Yes, I do too. I'm not—not a nice girl—not the kind of a woman you were willing to make such sacrifices for."

I said, "Now listen, Ruth, there are a lot of things you don't have to talk about. I'm not a fool. I know that you must have had a key to Arthur Gell's apartment. I knew that you were jealous of the blonde. I didn't figure you went up there just to pass the time of day with him. He'd been stepping around with this blonde, and you wanted a showdown. I knew all that before I ever got into this thing. So forget it."

"But, Donald, can't you understand? I'm—I'm putty as far as men are concerned."

"Who," I asked, "told you so?"

"Jim Laustan."

"And who," I asked, "is Jim Laustan?"

"The man I was engaged to."

"What happened to the engagement?"

"He broke it off."

"Why?"

"He—he—" Tears got the best of her. I patted her hip soothingly and let her bawl.

After a while, I said, "He told you you were a nymphomaniac?"

I could feel her head bobbing up and down against the lapel of my coat.

"Who," I asked, "was the first man in your life?"

"He was."

"Jim?"

I put my hands on her shoulders and tried to pull her away so I could look in her face, but she wriggled free to hold her head tight against my shoulder. "I can't t-t-talk if you're l-l-l-looking at me," she said.

"Look here, Ruth," I demanded. "Is this a gag?"

"No, I'm telling you the truth."

"Well, tell no more of it then."

"Jim said he couldn't marry me, that I couldn't—couldn't control myself."

"Nice of Jim," I said. "And did he sell you on the idea?"

"Donald, I'm bad. I'm wicked. I haven't been able to keep things—well, the way they should be. I was Arthur's girl. You know what I mean. I was—I gave myself to him."

"For money?" I asked.

She straightened up to stare at me with indignation in her eyes. "Why, Donald, how *dare* you say such a thing?"

"I didn't say it," I said. "I asked it."

"Of course not."

"And how many men have you been intimate with in this wildly checkered career of yours?" I asked.

She ducked for cover again. "Four," she said in a mumbled confession from the shoulder.

"Cheer up," I said. "I know a girl who had a record of five, and she got married and lived happily ever afterwards."

"Donald," she said, sulkily, "you're kidding me."

"Aren't you kidding me?"

"No, of course not."

"You know, Ruth," I said, "you're not living back in the Victorian era now. We've been discovering things about biology lately. Girls are human. We didn't admit it for a good many years, but now occasionally someone advances the idea."

"Oh, Donald, don't joke about it."

"Haven't you had any girlfriends?" I asked.

"Not—not since I knew Jim."

"Why not?"

"I was ashamed to—I don't know. The girls I'd known were all nice girls and—Donald, I tell you I *am* abnormal. I can't resist men. You know, not certain ones."

"You've resisted me all right—so far."

"You—you do the resisting."

I settled down to business then, and drew the story out of her. When I'd finished, I couldn't tell whether Jim Laustan had given her a line because he wanted to get rid of her, or whether he was one of those sanctimonious hypocrites who, having betrayed a girl into "sin," couldn't rid himself of the notion that she was a "soiled dove."

The girl had a goofy background. Her parents had died when she was a kid. She'd been in a convent, and then had gone to an uncle in the Middle West. He was a sourpuss whose idea of life, biology, and agriculture had been acquired somewhere around 1890, encrusted with a hard shell of resistance to all forms of change, and hermetically sealed against the infiltration of new ideas.

Ruth had come to the city about a year before. The new environment, the new sense of freedom, new ideas, and new emotions had resulted in "betrayal." Then, once awakened, she'd tried to put herself back to sleep, and hadn't been able to make the grade. A book, published around 1900, which purported to convey the facts of life and which she'd picked up in a secondhand bookstore, had completed the job. A green kid, an introvert, lonely in a city, without friends, sold on the idea she was abnormally sexed, she'd surrendered herself to a terminology she'd picked up in a secondhand bookstore—and Cunner, masquerading as Gell in a happy-go-lucky existence which brought him in a lot of easy money with no responsibility, had dated her up for dinner a couple of times, taken her dancing, capitalized on her loneliness, and found her a pushover.

And there she was, sitting on my lap, soaking my left coat lapel and shoulder with tears, a nervous, highly sexed bundle of feminine energy—accused of murder, and I was her accomplice.

I patted her shoulder and said, "All right, Ruth. Here's the sketch. We've stumbled into a nest of political graft. I know too much, and you know too much. They want us out of the way. A murder's been committed, and they need a fall guy for the murder. You can see where that leaves us. Now, they're building up a case against us which we'll never be able to beat, no matter what we say or what we do. We have only one chance—to find the real murderer and pin the crime on him before they frame us with it."

"Yes, dear," she said. "I know, honey, I thought for a while I was just a fallen woman and let it go at that, but since I've met you, I've realized how important it is to have a man's respect. I want you to understand if you can.—Oh, Donald, I'm not *all* bad."

"Okay, baby," I said, "you're not all bad. Now let's forget about your sex life for a minute and get down to brass tacks. What numbers did Arthur Gell habitually call on the telephone?"

"Not very many. Most of the calls were to him."

"He used to call that blonde?"

"Yes."

"And you used to listen in?"

She avoided my eyes. I gave her a quick shake, and said, "For Christ's sake, snap out of it! You listened in, didn't you?"

"Yes."

"What did they say?"

"It was some sort of a code, a lot of things about members and forms and dates."

"Can you give me a sample of it?"

"Not to repeat her exact language, but it would go something like this. She'd say, 'On the sixteenth, they're using form four. I have three at fifty dollars and two at a hundred.' And he'd say, 'That's too cheap. Can't you boost them to a hundred and a hundred and fifty?' And she'd say, 'No, I did the best I could.'—You know, Donald, it would go something like that."

I pinched my brows together and tried to think. She was heavy on my lap. I said, "Go over and sit on that chair, Ruth, and let me try to figure this thing out."

"What is there to figure?"

"The blonde," I said, "undoubtedly was giving him the dope on the examinations, the date when they'd come up, what form they'd be using, and the number of people she'd lined up who would pay money for the answers. Don't you see?"

"I guess so, yes.—Donald, why don't you want me to sit on your lap? Is it because you've lost respect for me?"

"It's because you're so damn heavy," I said. "Now tell me, do you know anything about the name Cerfitone?"

"I've read it somewhere or heard it."

"Did Gell ever call Cerfitone over the telephone?"

"I don't know.—Donald, do you think I'm brazen and no good?"

"You're a nice kid," I said, absent-mindedly patting her leg, my mind on Cerfitone. "Suppose you take a look in the telephone directory, Ruth, find Cerfitone's number, and see if that means anything to you."

"It wouldn't. I'm not much at remembering numbers.—Oh, Donald, I thrill so when you touch me."

"Can you remember the blonde's number?" I asked.

"I'll never forget *that*," she said savagely.

I said, "Well, that gives us one break. What's the number?"

"Westmore 69021. Donald, do you know something?"

"What?"

"Last night when we were out in the car, you kissed me, and seemed to—seemed to like it. Now, since I've told you about—about—about you know what—you haven't offered to kiss me a single time. I know it's because you've lost your respect—"

I picked her up, walked across to the davenport with her. She looked over her shoulder to see where I was going, twisted her arm around my neck, and pressed the circle of her lips close against mine.

I dumped her on the davenport, picked up the telephone, and called Westmore 69021.

She lay there, watching me with wide, anxious eyes, lying just as I'd dropped her, one knee cocked up, her eyes swollen from crying, but following my every move with an expression of anxiety.

After a while, a woman's voice said cautiously, "Hello."

"This is the Service Department at the Telephone Company," I said. "We're asking for an okay on the long-distance call which was placed from this number last night."

"What call?" the voice asked.

"A call to San Francisco, at Prospect 9654."

"You're sure it was from this number?" she asked.

"Yes," I said.

"I think there's some mistake. This is a private, unlisted telephone, and—"

"We understand all that," I interrupted. "The call was placed by a Ralph Cerfitone. He said that the phone wasn't registered in his name, but we could get an okay from the owner of the telephone."

"Oh," she said, "that's all right. I didn't know about the call, but it's okay."

"Very well," I said, keeping all the interest out of my voice. "We're checking just as a matter of routine. Now, am I talking with the person in whose name the telephone is registered?"

"That's right, yes."

"Your name, please?"

"Anita Premmer," she said.

"And the address?"

"Look here," she said. "You have all that, don't you, on your records?"

"Of course. I'm simply verifying that I'm talking with the owner of the telephone. It's a matter of routine."

There was sudden suspicion in her voice. She said, "Well, that's all the information you're going to get until I find out more about that call," and slammed the telephone receiver in my ear.

Hell, I should have known it all along. Gell was peddling information to parties who gave an okay by saying they came from Premmer. Naturally, we'd jumped at the conclusion that it was *Mr.* Premmer because he was in the Civil Service Department. But with an unidentified blonde in the background, we should have figured the play. I began to think that Bertha Cool had been stampeded pretty easily. But it was too late for that now.

Ruth Marr, from the davenport, said dreamily, "She *wasn't* his sister, was she, Donald?"

"No," I said, and rang the number of Bertha Cool's agency.

Elsie Brand answered the telephone. I raised the pitch of my voice as much as I could. "Is Mr. Lam in?" I asked.

"Mr. Lam is out on a case. We don't know just when he'll be back. Who is this talking please?"

"Mr. Smith," I said, "of Portland, Oregon. I wanted to see Mr. Lam."

"I'll tell him you called, Mr. Smith. Any message?"

"Yes, tell Donald that my wife is with me and is very anxious to see him."

"Your wife?—Oh, yes, Mr. Smith, I'll see that he gets the message, and, by the way, is your name James Walter Smith?"

I thought for a moment, and said, "Yes, that's the name."

"Mr. Lam wrote you a letter," she said. "He didn't know where to send it so it's at general delivery at the post office. You can get it there if you call."

"Thanks. And you have my message?"

"Yes, I'll see that it's delivered, Mr. Smith *and* Mrs. Smith."

"That's right."

She hung up. I turned to Ruth. "Okay, baby, I've got to go out and round up some stuff. It's dangerous. I'm going to give you a hundred and fifty bucks. Stick right close to the apartment. If you read in the papers that they've caught me, you'll have to try for a getaway. Don't use busses, planes, or trains. Use your sex appeal and hitchhike. Do you understand?"

"Oh, Donald, *don't* leave me."

"I have to," I said.

"Donald, come over here and sit down beside me, just for a minute."

She moved her legs to give me room on the davenport. I came over and sat down beside her. She played with the fingers of my right hand.

"You're so capable and manly and self-reliant, darling. I can't bear to think of being without you. I'll go crazy if you leave me here and—"

"Look here, Ruth," I said. "That's one thing I wanted to ask you, something I've forgotten in all the rush of excitement."

"What is it, honey?" she asked, her eyes holding mine.

"That man whom you saw coming out of Gell's apartment," I said. "I saw him when he went into the apartment house and again when he came out. There was something funny about his walk. I can't place exactly what it was—something about the way he handled his feet."

She frowned and said, absently, "I seem to remember something too.—Donald, do I have to stay here all alone tonight?"

"Snap out of it," I told her. "Get your mind focused on that person. What was it about his feet?"

She sighed tremulously. I could see the tips of pearly teeth through half-parted lips. Abruptly her eyes widened. She said, "*I* know what it was. It wasn't his feet. It was his pants."

"What about his pants?"

"They weren't pegged, Donald, and they were funny."

"Not all pants are pegged," I said.

"I know, I know, but this was something—I'll tell you what it was. They'd been tucked in at the bottom and basted up around the inside. You know, Donald, I've seen men in clothing stores trying on suits, and they'd walk just like that. The salesman turn the pants up on the inside, and put pins in them, and—"

I grabbed her shoulders enthusiastically. "Baby, you've got it. Hot dog! We're on the right track. We've got it now, the whole thing!"

"What do you mean, Donald?"

"The whole damn thing," I said. "It's a cinch."

I grabbed my hat.

"Donald," she called softly.

"Remember what I told you," I said, heading for the door. "Stick close to the apartment. If they catch me, take it on the lam."

"Donald, I may not see you again. Oh, Donald—"

I opened the door and called back over my shoulder, "I think that's the best tour, Mademoiselle. I'll try and get the tickets."

I slammed the door shut behind me and sprinted.

I was getting into the elevator by the time she'd opened the door to stand watching me silently. I jumped inside and pressed the button. The sliding door slowly closed, and the elevator wheezed downward.

I figured a taxicab would get me to the post office quicker than getting the agency car out of the parking lot. I hailed a cab and made time. General delivery window was still open, and I didn't even have to hand out a line by way of identifying myself. I simply asked in a bored voice for Smith—James Walter, and took the letter which the clerk handed me with an air of bored resignation, waited for a moment to see if there was anything else, thanked him, and walked over to a corner of the post office. I tore open the envelope, took out the typewritten sheet of stationery, and read, "The gun that you inquired about was a thirty-eight Smith & Wesson, police-positive. It was sold to Eben Cunner approximately two months ago. He purchased three guns, all of the same make, model, and caliber, and all at the same time. Because of his connection with Webley & McMarr he got them wholesale. Evidently you're on the trail of something. Don't hold out any information. Let me know what you have."

The letter was unsigned. I tore it and the envelope into tiny bits and dropped them in the big, iron receptacle used for wastepaper, and then walked over to stand by the desk with its sputtery, corroded pens and thin blotting paper while I smoked a cigarette and thought.

Bertha Cool would get my message about Mrs. Smith. She'd know then that I'd located the blonde. She'd wait at the office for me to call. It was a question whether I dared to call. We were dealing with crooked police and political graft. Their first move would be to tap the telephone line.

I smoked halfway through a cigarette, debating whether it would be better to write her a special delivery or send her a telegram. I finally decided on the telegram. I knew there was a telegraph office down the street. I pushed my way through the swinging door of the post office and started walking briskly through the late afternoon crowds.

There was an alley intersection by the post office with no signal. A car was coming through just as I stepped off the curb. I waited for it to pass. A door opened. I got a flashing glimpse of a gold star pinned to a vest. A man's voice said, "Well, you managed to keep under cover pretty well, didn't you, Donald?"

A big arm snaked out and caught me by the top of the vest. I tried to jerk loose. A man jumped out from the front seat and grabbed my elbow.

They were officers all right. Their stars were even stuck on the outside of their coats. As I was lifted into the car, I heard the man who had been in the front seat growl at the startled spectators, "Just a routine arrest. Keep moving. Don't block the sidewalk."

The car lurched into motion. Just for good measure, a siren cut into action.

I settled back against the cushions, and said, "Okay, take me to headquarters, and I want a lawyer."

I heard a scornful laugh on my left. A man's voice said, "You get that, Bill? He wants to go to headquarters."

I'd heard that voice before. I looked up over my left shoulder.

It was the face of Alfred, the man who had smacked me over the head with the gun barrel at the Orange Cove Apartments.

There was a traffic cop at the intersection, standing to one side and holding up traffic for the siren. I tried to yell at him. A fist caught me in the stomach. Something hard clipped me on the back of the ear. I went down into the bottom of the car. A heel of a shoe pressed down against my lips. A man's voice, sounding distinctly ominous, said, "Stay there, you little son of a bitch."

I felt the heel pressing my lips against my teeth. My nose was filled with the smell of leather. Dirt ground against my teeth and into my mouth. I couldn't get my breath. I twisted my head sideways to get out from under the pressure of that heel.

Somebody kicked me just back of the ear, and I passed out.

Chapter X.

I regained consciousness with the sound of voices in my ears, voices that swelled into sound, receded and then boomed back into noise like the pound of distant surf on a coral reef.

I was only dimly conscious of the ache in my head. I was primarily concerned in fighting for breath. My hands were tied so I couldn't reach at the gag which had been stuffed into my mouth, and I was barely getting enough air to keep from strangling.

For what seemed hours, I tried to time my breathing so I could get enough air to keep alive. Before I could get my lungs fully filled, I had to exhale. Before I could get the dead air out, I was fighting to get fresh air in.

For a long time, the sounds I heard didn't mean anything.

Then I became aware that the sounds were words and the words conveyed ideas, although the meaning seemed impersonal and detached despite the fact that it concerned my life.

A man, speaking in well-modulated tones, seemed to be very much put out. There was an accentless quality in the speech that enabled me to identify the voice. It was that of the well-dressed man in the gray suit with the pearl-gray tie. He said, "You damn fools need a guardian. Don't you know that those ropes will leave marks that will be visible at the post-mortem, and that gag—how the hell are we going to make it look like a hit-and-run case with the marks of ropes on his arms and a gag in his mouth?—Give me that knife.—He'll stay unconscious until we get ready to dump him. He's a frail little drink of water.

Why tie him up? If he comes to, we can beat him back to sleep. Here, give me that knife."

I felt a crushing weight on my chest, then cold steel along the back of my neck. By an effort I managed to remain limp and motionless.

The knife cut through the cloth gag. I felt it loosen, and it took all of my control to keep from sucking in a lungful of fresh air. I managed to breathe slowly and evenly.

"Jesus," he said, "he's half blue already. You smother him with that gag, and then try to make it look like an accident. God, if I could only get someone who had half the intelligence of a medium-sized canary bird. I don't mind having to work with rats, but I'd like to find someone with a quarter of the sense that God gave a half-grown, reasonably well-nourished rat."

The knife cut through the ropes that held my wrists. I could feel blood tingling into my numbed fingertips as though an electric battery was pouring current into my arms.

Above me the tirade went on and on, a monologue of well-modulated accusation and abuse.

No one tried to answer him. I couldn't tell whether he was talking to one person or half a dozen.

"All right, fools, dumbbells," he said angrily, "give me a hand. Get him in this car. Cover him with this robe.—Now get the hell out and build alibis for yourselves."

Alfred's voice said, "Better let me go, boss, in case you need—"

"Don't be a damn fool," came the interruption of that cold, accentless voice. "The more men, the more alibis we have to fake. Get out and get on the job. Scatter. Leave this little runt to me. He isn't any bigger than a second hand on a lady's wrist-watch.—And, Christ, look at the trouble he's caused. Well, he's all washed up now. He'll return to the scene of the crime, prowling around the Mountain Crest Apartments, and some hit-and-run driver will knock him into the morgue. That's all there'll be to it."

Hands clutched at my shoulders, at my ankles. I was lifted and tossed into an automobile. The jar of hitting the floor of the automobile sent me back into oblivion.

When I came to again, there was no noise save the rumble of the running gear as the tires rolled along the paved highway. That rumble was magnified by my aching head until it felt as though a pneumatic riveter was at work on my brain.

I lay there, taking stock of the situation. Because I've always been too small to put up much of a fight, I've developed a general technique of fighting. It's conserve your energy, play a waiting game, never hit until you can land a knockout, and when you do hit, have no rules of sportsmanship to hamper your technique. Don't use your fist, if a club's handy. Don't use a club, if there's a gun.

Bertha Cool says I have a warped disposition, that I'm plain poison.

Well, this was the end of the trail. I was nauseated from the beatings I'd received, and just about half conscious. If I'd been fully conscious, I couldn't have done anything. At the first move from me, the driver would turn around, smack me with a slung shot as casually as he'd have hit a fly with a flyswatter. I'd have gone back down with a fractured skull. I'd been beaten, pummeled, kicked, and clubbed. I'd dabbled with crooked politics and had lost out. I was holding the short end of the ticket. The telephone line to Bertha Cool's office had been tapped, of course. They'd been waiting for me when I picked up the letter at general delivery. I knew the chances I'd been taking. Bertha Cool had warned me of them, but I'd wanted that letter. What the hell. I'd taken a gamble and lost.

I couldn't have mustered enough strength to have struggled free of the folds of that automobile robe even if I'd known I could have caught the driver unawares. I was in that border state between consciousness and unconsciousness which is like the few minutes before slumber comes at night or wakefulness in the morning. My mind was a warped lens projecting a distorted image on the screen of my consciousness. I knew it was the end. In one way I didn't care. I'd absorbed too much of a beating to want to fight back. My bruised body only wanted rest. Physically, I was licked. Mentally, I wasn't. I wanted revenge. I knew I was going, but I wanted to take this guy with me. I found myself wishing my skin was stuffed with nitroglycerin, that I had some way of exploding myself and taking us all into eternity. I couldn't plan intelligently because my mind wasn't functioning clearly enough, but I did make up my mind that when he stopped the car and opened the door to take me out, I'd feign unconsciousness until the last, and trust that I could drive my heel into his chin hard enough to give me a chance.

It was just an idle dream. After what seemed a succession of jolting hours, the car came to a stop. The door opened. I felt hands tugging at the auto robe. Then a hand caught my leg and jerked. My head hit something, and the blackness of unconsciousness engulfed me.

It was the fresh air and the cold pavement which brought me to. I could hear the steady chirp of frogs in a pool somewhere nearby. The stars were blazing down with calm splendor. The night air was cool and bracing, and the oiled surface of the road was like a cake of ice.

A car was standing in the center of the road facing me. The headlights were glaring into my tortured eyes. A tall figure was walking away from me, toward the car.

I lunged forward and up. I tried to take a swift, running step. My knees buckled. I came down in a heap.

I saw the silhouetted figure against the headlights turn, start running toward me.

I knew I couldn't trust my legs. I threw myself in a twisting headlong spin which sent me rolling dizzily down the banked roadway into the deep ditch.

I had a hazy second of unconsciousness. Then, above me, I saw a figure bending down. I could hear the rattle of loose rocks sliding down the steep grade of the embankment.

I tried to close my right hand into a fist. The fingers were clutching a rock.

The man bent over me. I could hear his heavy breathing. He raised his arm.

I flung the rock.

The expenditure of energy was too much for me. I went into the blackness again.

I don't know when it was that I regained consciousness. Dew had commenced to form. My hair was damp. The rocks were slimed with moisture. A weight lay across my waist, a weight which pinned me down.

I felt stronger now. I struggled to a sitting position. The weight was that of the inert body of the man who had taken me for a ride.

I thought at first he was dead and acted on that assumption. After a while, when I got strong enough to roll him off my legs, I felt for a pulse. There was a thin, barely perceptible throb at his wrist.

I fished through his pockets and found a flashlight. There was a gun in a shoulder holster under his left armpit. I turned on the flashlight. It was the man in gray. My rock had struck him on the left temple. There was a big, bruised welt from which blood was slowly seeping. His face was almost without color.

I went through his pockets. The driving license and cards

showed he was Ralph Cerfitone. He had money in his wallet, something over a thousand dollars.

According to the rules of fair fighting, I should have left the money. To hell with that stuff. I don't fight fair. The money represented sinews of war. No one had been particularly ethical with me. I stripped every dollar out of the wallet. Sitting there in the cool of the mountain night, I began to feel stronger. I slipped the gun out of the holster. Its weight was reassuring. I snuggled the butt into my hand, and then realized that it was a thirty-eight caliber Smith & Wesson police-positive. The flashlight confirmed the impression.

I guess my brains were really woozy from the beatings I'd received. The significance of the gun didn't register with me. I pushed it into my hip pocket and got to my feet.

Getting up that embankment was a major job.

The road was a mountain road which ran up to some cabins. At this season of the year, it was practically unused except for Sunday picnickers. Cerfitone's automobile still stood in the center of the road, the motor idling. God knows how long it had been there.

I climbed in and got the feel of the wheel and gear shift. I eased in the clutch and started driving straight ahead without having any clear idea of where I was going. After a while, I came to a boulevard stop and saw lights to the right. I turned right, and the Mountain Crest Apartments came into view with its blood-red neon sign blazing against the white stars.

Not until then did I get the idea.

I stopped the car to think it over. I took out the gun and looked at it. Undoubtedly, it was one of the three guns Cunner had bought wholesale. Evidently, he'd wanted one for himself and one apiece for two friends. Cerfitone had been one of the "friends." The guns were identical except for numbers—

I drove the car down to the crossroad where I'd hid the

murder gun. I dug out the gun, slipped the exploded shell out of the cylinder, and put in a fresh shell from Cerfitone's gun. I drove back to where I'd left Cerfitone. He was still unconscious, still breathing. I slipped the murder gun into his shoulder holster and drove away.

Chapter XI.

Bertha Cool answered my knock on the door of her apartment.

She was clad in heavy silk pajamas which showed lots of her anatomy, both by clinging to the contours as well as through semitransparency. Seen in that garb, she didn't look out of proportion, only big, massive, and powerful. She didn't bulge and sag with soft fat, but was a huge power plant, immune to such human things as worry, fatigue, or despondency.

Her breath smelled of whiskey, but her eyes were cold, clear, and hard.

"My God, what's happened to *you!*" she said. "Well, come on in. Don't stand there gawking."

I came in. She slammed the door and locked it, stood entirely without self-consciousness, looking me over, from the cut on the top of my head to the dust on my feet.

"My God, Donald," she said, "don't you know better than to come *here*? Of all the asinine things you've ever done, this takes the cake."

"They're not looking for me anymore," I said.

"Don't kid yourself they aren't. That's a way they have for trapping suckers. They pretend to relax their vigilance and—"

"They think I'm dead," I said.

She said, "Oh," walked across to the chair in front of the smoking stand, picked up the glass of whiskey and soda, and said, "Sit down."

I went over to a chair and dropped.

She said, "I suppose you could use a jolt of whiskey?"

I said, "I suppose I could."

She tossed off the whiskey and soda in her glass, and splashed straight Scotch into the tumbler. She got up from the chair as easily as though she'd only weighed a hundred and ten pounds and carried the glass across to me. "Drink as much as you need," she said. "Don't get drunk.—There aren't any germs on the glass.—If there are, the whiskey will kill 'em."

I drank about half of the glass of whiskey before I felt a choking sensation in my throat, and handed the balance back to her. I pulled out a bloody handkerchief and coughed into it.

She looked at the whiskey in the tumbler as though debating whether to dilute it with soda, then tossed if off neat, and walked back to her chair. She said, "Take your time, Donald. Wait until the whiskey takes effect. Don't hurry. Tell Bertha all about it."

After a while, I said, "Ralph Cerfitone is the guy who's behind the thing. Judge Carter Longan is laying for him. He'll play ball with us if we want to bring things to a showdown."

"We don't want to bring things to a showdown," she said. "Bertha wants to cut herself a slice of cake."

I closed my eyes and didn't argue about it. The whiskey was warming up my gullet, sending warm life chasing the coldness of collapse out of my veins.

"Where have you been, Donald?" she asked.

"Taken for a ride," I said.

She thought that over for a while, then asked casually, "They got you, I suppose, when you called for that letter?"

I nodded.

"It was a damn fool thing to do," she said. "Elsie should have known better than to have told you over the telephone. The line was tapped."

"How else could she have told me?" I asked.

"She could have been a little more subtle about it."

"Well, that's water under the bridge now."

Bertha heaved a sigh, elevated her thick, powerful legs to an ottoman, crossed her ankles, looked at the half-empty whiskey bottle as though debating whether to have another drink, and then decided on a cigarette instead. "Want a cigarette, Donald?" she asked.

"Not now," I said.

"Well," she observed, "they didn't mark your face up much. Now you're getting some color back, you don't look so bad. I suppose your body is sore. You move as though it was."

"It is."

She looked me over again, and shook her head dubiously. "You're a little runt to be out on the firing line, Donald, but you do have guts and intelligence. Elsie tells me you've located the blonde."

I nodded.

"Who is it?"

"Mrs. Premmer," I said.

Bertha Cool sat upright, staring at me with cold, steady eyes. Then she began to curse under her breath, a low monotone of heartfelt profanity.

"What's the matter?" I asked.

"Don't pay any attention to me, Donald. I'm cussing me, not you. Of all the damn stupidity.—Christ, I should have known— certainly let myself get pushed into a corner easy.—Jesus, Donald, I must be getting old or soft or something.—Tell me, Donald does *he* know?"

"No, I don't think so."

"No," she said, after a moment's thoughtful silence, "he wouldn't. That's the only way he could have put the act across with me. If he'd known, I'd have smelled that knowledge. It was his indignant sincerity that sent me hunting for cover. How did you find out, lover?"

"It's a long story."

"Tell it to me."

"I'd rather not."

"You have to, Donald."

I said, "I went to see Judge Longan."

"He didn't tell you, did he?"

"No."

"Give you any clue?"

"Not directly. He was gunning for Cerfitone."

"What does he know about Cerfitone?"

"Not enough. He knows generally what's going on in the Civil Service. He's interested. I don't think he has any proof—just suspicions. He didn't talk. He listened."

"Yes," she said musingly, "he would."

"I have a hunch he's been investigating the thing from another angle. This tied in with something else he knows. He was a lot more interested than he would have been if the idea had been thrown at him out of a clear sky."

Bertha said, "We're not in business for our health, Donald. We're not going to hand Judge Longan anything on a silver platter."

"We may not be in business for our health," I said bitterly, "but we've got to watch our step if we want to keep our health."

She wagged her head slowly from side to side and said, "You shouldn't have gone after that letter—not after the way Elsie spilled the beans over the telephone."

I kept silent, feeling the whiskey doing its stuff. The warmth of the apartment felt good after the cold night air.

"How about that girl, Donald?" she asked abruptly.

"What girl?" I asked.

She said, "Don't try to hand Bertha a line, Donald. Kick through and tell her about the girl."

"You mean the blonde?"

"Christ, no. I mean Ruth Marr. Snap out of it, Donald, and give Bertha the lowdown."

"I don't know as there is any. She hasn't been picked up by the police, has she?"

"You know she hasn't."

"She's a good kid," I defended.

"She was laying up with Cunner, Donald. Epsworth, the night clerk, had caught her at it. She didn't know that he knew."

"Listen," I said hotly, "she's a good kid. She came from the country. She'd been brought up in an environment where she knew little about life and nothing about sex. She came to the city, and they took her."

Bertha Cool heaved a sigh which might as well have been a yawn, and said, "Uh huh. I've heard *that* story before."

"This time it happens to be true."

"Nuts," she said. "It's never true. A girl sometimes gets seduced before she knows what it's all about. By the time the first man gets done with her, she knows.—I don't think Cunner was the first man, not by a damn sight."

"If you are interested in statistics," I said weakly, "he was the fourth."

"How old is she?"

"Twenty-three or four."

"The fourth," Bertha said. "Humph!"

I opened my eyes and said irritably, "For Christ's sake, leave her out of this."

"She's in," Bertha said.

"Well, you and I'll leave her out."

"Where are you keeping her, Donald?"

"I'm not keeping her," I said.

"Don't lie to Bertha, Donald, because Bertha has ways of finding things out."

"Go ahead and find out then," I said, "and quit asking me questions."

"What time is it, Donald?"

"I don't know. My wristwatch is broken."

She said, "My watch is in the bathroom," seemed to debate with herself whether she should go and get it, noticed the telephone. She picked it up, called time information, said, "Thank you," hung up, and said to me, "It's twelve minutes and forty seconds past eleven."

I nodded wearily. Time didn't mean a great deal to me.

"What did you come here for, Donald?"

I said, "We've got to get a showdown on this thing before morning. We have enough to go on now. We can't sit back and let them push us around."

She studied me thoughtfully. "Feel up to it, Donald?"

"I will in a minute."

"Want another drink of whiskey?"

"No."

She said, "I guess we have to call on the Premmers."

I said, "Naturally. What did you think I came here for?"

She said, "Don't be sarcastic, lover. You've dealt me a lot of low cards.—They'll find out you've been here."

"Who will?"

"The ring that's running this thing. This afternoon, you were the only one that had the information. They could bump you off and take a chance on getting by. Now that you've found out about Mrs. Premmer and have come here, they'll have to kill us both if they want to bottle up the information."

I was too tired to even nod my head. I let it sink back against the cushions of the chair.

She said, musingly, "I'll take a hell of a lot more killing than you will, Donald."

"I'm still here," I said indignantly.

"Yes," she said thoughtfully, "and that's all."

After a minute, I said, "Well, what do you want to do?"

"Donald," she said, "you have to put on evening clothes."

"Evening clothes?"

"Yes."

"You mean a tuxedo?"

"Hell, no. I mean tails, a top hat, white gloves, a gardenia, the whole damned outfit."

"You're crazy," I said.

"No, I'm not crazy. It'll be eleven-thirty before we can get there. Try to bust in like that and we'd be on our way to the morgue by midnight.—But who the hell ever heard of a detective wandering around in tails?—No, Donald, there's an outfitter in this block. He's a friend of mine. He was a client once. That was before he got his divorce. He's married now, a cute little trick who used to work for him in the front office. He'll come up, Donald, measure you. They keep open until one-thirty, not so much to send out suits as to get them back. He likes to get them back the same night wherever possible. He's a canny Scotchman. You'll like him.—No, you won't either. You don't have enough vitality to like anyone who's continually trying to put you on the defensive.—I'll call him."

She picked up the telephone and dialed a number. After a while, she said, "Let me talk with Angus," then after a few moments, "Angus, this is Bertha Cool. Come up here. I have a job for you.—No, a job.—Yes, up here.—Now.—For Christ's sake, Angus, don't try to pull that line with me. When I tell you

I have a job for you, I mean I have a job for you. When I say come up here, I mean come up here.—No, I don't know what time it is, and I don't give a damn. A few minutes ago, it was twelve minutes and forty seconds past eleven. It's later than that now, and I don't give a damn how much later. You can make it up here in three minutes if you hurry. Hurry."

She hung up the telephone without waiting to hear anything more and without saying goodbye. She opened the drawer in her desk, took out her long cigarette holder, and with some difficulty fitted the moist end of the cigarette into the end of the holder. "Christ," she said, apropos of nothing, "I get tired of men who want to argue all the time."

I felt the warmth of the apartment on my skin, the warmth of the whiskey in my veins. The cushions of the chair were soft. I kept my eyes closed, thought I should say something, but couldn't think of just what I should say. A delicious drowsiness crept over me.

The sound of voices wakened me. They seemed to have been going on for some time. I heard Bertha Cool's voice break through the languor of fatigue. "—no, he doesn't have to stand up. Run your tape measure up under his coat."

I heard a man's voice grumble something in an undertone, and Bertha Cool say, "Jesus Christ, do I have to hit you with a club every time I want something? You know damn well, Angus, that all I have to do is to give a certain party a hint of what I know, and you'd be on the inside looking out."

I heard the sound of swift motion, heard the man say something in a whisper, heard Bertha Cool go on, in the same even voice, "God knows I hate to have to do it, but you keep asking for it. You never will be properly polite about things. I have to beat you over the head with a club in order to let any sense in. For Christ's sake, get those measurements, and then get down and send up the clothes. Don't tell me you can't do it because you can. Measure his sleeves. Measure his pants. Measure his neck.—No, we aren't going to get blood on your white shirt front, and if we do, it'll launder off. Get busy."

I tried to wake up enough to at least register a protest to the hands which did things to me, but the whiskey had sent alcoholic fumes into my brain, and I didn't have enough resistance to cope with them. I was warm and tired—awfully tired.

After a while, the hands quit tugging at me. I had a short period of restful oblivion, and then Bertha Cool was pulling my pants off. "Come on, Donald," she said. "Snap into it. We haven't got all night. Here, Angus, get that shirt off."

They got me up on my feet. The light hurt my eyes. I had a hard time standing still, but gradually I fought off the lassitude so that I could help them. Bertha Cool said, "There you are, lover. You'll have to button up the pants in front. Bertha will make a nice neat job with the tie. You can carry the hat in your hand if it hurts your head to put it on."

Angus was a short, stubby man with a cold eye and a bulldog jaw. He was thick of shoulder and chest, heavy of waist, but not fat. His fingers were powerful, stubby, and active. He acted as though he was frightened to death. The grumble had gone out of his voice, and he was almost servile when he said anything to Bertha. For the most part, she didn't give him an opportunity to say anything. She told him.

They had me dressed after a while and after a fashion. I felt better going down the stairs, and then Bertha summoned a taxicab.

"How'd you get here, Donald?" she asked, as the cab driver held the door open.

"I stole the car they used in taking me for a ride. I think it belonged to the guy whose name I mentioned."

"You didn't park it near here?"

"Two or three blocks away," I said.

She said, "Hell, Donald, that's bad. We should have moved it."

"No use now," I said. "It's whole hog or nothing."

I felt the taxi sway as Bertha Cool's weight pulled the springs far over to one side. "Don't you worry, lover," she said reassuringly, the body of the taxicab rocking violently back and forth as she adjusted herself into a comfortable position, "it'll be the whole hog with Bertha."

"Where to?" the cab driver asked.

Bertha snapped a street number at him. I presumed she'd looked up Premmer's address, or else she knew it already. I settled back to another period of restful inactivity.

After a while, I heard Bertha Cool saying tartly, "And don't look at me like that, my man. Ten cents is plenty for a tip. The way business conditions are now, you're goddamn lucky to get that. Come on, Donald."

I'd been left sitting there while Bertha Cool got out and paid off the taxi. I could see that the taxi driver thought I was drunk, which was all right by me.

There was a night clerk on duty in the apartment house. Bertha Cool beamed at him with her best dowager air. She looked very stately and dignified in a light-colored creation that was full of satiny sheen with a transparent lacy effect minimizing the huge expanse of her chest and the powerful muscles of her straight back. "Tell Mrs. Premmer that we've just dropped in from the opera," she said, "and must see her at once on a matter of the greatest importance. Tell her it's Bertha calling." She flashed the diamonds at him and smiled.

There was a doo-dad on the telephone which enabled the

clerk to talk into the mouthpiece without his conversation being audible to the persons who stood at the desk. For a moment, he seemed to have a bit of an argument, but he didn't ask us any more questions. The full dress put it across just as Bertha had figured it would. He talked and listened, then talked some more, listened and smiled affably at us. "You may go up," he said. "It's apartment B on the twelfth floor."

The elevator boy seemed duly impressed by our correct attire. He shot us up to the twelfth. Bertha Cool took the lead and barged down the corridor toward the mahogany door which had "B" stamped on it in gold leaf.

It was the blonde all right. I knew her the moment she opened the door, even before my eyes came to a sharp focus on her. She was wearing a long, dark formal. Her breasts were beautiful, and the gown barely covered just what the law would require having covered. There was puzzled perplexity in her eyes and in the sudden parting of her lips as she saw Bertha Cool and me standing on the threshold.

Bertha Cool moved forward.

There was nothing ostentatious about it, certainly nothing violent, but it was as irresistible as the progress of a steam roller. Before the firm finality of that approach, the blonde fell back into the room.

Bertha Cool, beaming, held out a diamond-encrusted hand in greeting. She was halfway into the room before the blonde got her breath enough to say, "Won't—won't you come in?"

Bertha Cool took the blonde's hand, and said, "So glad to meet you, Mrs. Premmer," looked around with a motherly eye, and said, "Sit down over on that chair, Donald. It's the most comfortable one. Just relax and take it easy."

Bertha Cool smiled affably at her surprised hostess, and said, "And if you'll pardon me, Mrs. Premmer, I'll take the most substantial chair. I like substantial chairs. How about it, Donald? Is this the woman?"

"That's the woman," I said, sitting down and relaxing.

Bertha Cool positively beamed effusive cordiality. "I'm Bertha Cool," she said. "This is Donald."

The blonde looked at me, her manner hard, suspicious, and poised as a cat looks on an approaching dog from the vantage point of a fence post. "I've seen you before somewhere," she said.

Bertha Cool said, "Tell her, Donald."

"I'm a detective," I said. "I followed you when you went out with Cunner.—You knew him as Gell. I'm Donald Lam."

Mrs. Premmer stiffened and said, "I certainly don't know to what you are referring. If this is some form of blackmail, you may as well understand now as later that you're wasting your effort. I have no secrets from my husband. I have his perfect confidence. Will you please state the nature of your errand?"

I said, somewhat wearily, "Oh, don't try the high-and-mighty act. There are too many people who can identify you, the night clerk at the Mountain Crest for one, the garage man for the other."

I was dog tired. I knew I'd made a mistake as soon as I mentioned that about the garage man. That's why Cunner had never taken her into the garage with him, but had picked up the car and met her out on the road to the apartment. I saw hard triumph in her eyes.

"For your information," she said, "I am quite certain that the night clerk at the Mountain Crest Apartments will say that he has never seen me before, because I have no knowledge of having seen him, and, as far as any garage men are concerned, I don't know what you're talking about. My husband has already been annoyed by a blackmailing detective agency. While, of course, I have no way of knowing, I presume that you represent the same agency. I am going to ask you to terminate this visit at once. Otherwise, I shall call the police."

"Listen," I said, "you went out to the Yucca Club with Cunner. You sat there at the bar while you drank some cocktails, and then—"

Mrs. Premmer spun toward the telephone. I had a chance to study the smooth lines of her figure flowing gracefully underneath the thin cloth of the dress. She picked up the telephone and said icily, "Will you leave, or shall I call the police? You have just ten seconds to decide."

Bertha Cool said amiably, "Now just sit right back and relax, Donald. Don't strain yourself with a lot of unnecessary effort. You just leave this bitch to me."

Mrs. Premmer almost dropped the telephone. "What did you say?" she asked. "*What* was that word?"

"Bitch," Bertha Cool said, "b-i-t-c-h, dearie. It means slut. In this particular case, a two-timing tart who was acting as go-between in the sale of Civil Service examination questions. Now sit down, dearie, and take a load off your feet before Bertha has to help you to a chair."

I could see the woman's face losing color.

"My husband will be here soon. He'll put you in your place."

"No husband ever has so far," Bertha Cool remarked affably. "I don't know how well you thought you were covering your tracks, but Donald here got a good look at you. I suppose you're standing in with the night clerk at the apartment, but don't forget the girl at the telephone desk, dearie. She has no reason to lie awake nights worrying about any trouble you're going to get into."

"*That* woman," Mrs. Premmer said. "I think I know now what

you have reference to. I read about it in the newspaper. She was, I believe, the—mistress of the man who was killed. But then, I suppose all telephone girls are promiscuous, aren't they?"

"Well, why not?" Bertha Cool asked affably. "The fact that she was laying up with Gell doesn't let *you* out. I don't suppose it's ever occurred to you that you've left fingerprints all over the apartment and over the Gell car—Jesus Christ, if I have to spell it out for you, your fingerprints are all over the perforated silk examination masks that you were dishing out to the various firemen and speed cops who wanted to take the examinations. That's better, dearie. Put that phone down and take a load off your feet. You and Bertha are going to talk business."

Mrs. Premmer moved her hand away from the telephone as though her fingers were numb. She stared uncertainly at Bertha Cool for a moment, then sat down across from me, but her eyes didn't even flicker in my direction. They stared in steady fascination at Bertha.

"What—" she started to asked, and then as she realized how her voice sounded, backed up and tried again, "What do you want?"

Bertha Cool said, "I think, dearie, that if you'd just write it all out in your own handwriting and sign it, we might be able to keep you out of it—that is, publicly."

"You're crazy."

Bertha said, "It's past midnight, and I've got a lot of work to do tonight. You get the hell over to that desk and write out a confession. Don't go into a lot of unnecessary details, but give me the dope on how the cash was handled, what your cut was, how much Cerfitone got, and all the dope on the payoff."

"Why, I don't even know what you're talking about."

Bertha looked at her and said, in a tone of genuine boredom, "Christ, I hope I don't have to get rough with you. You've got a cute little figure, but you'd mess easy."

Mrs. Premmer tried a flash of defiance. "If I understand the situation correctly," she said, "this is Mr. Donald Lam who is being sought by the police. They have an excellent murder case against him."

"That's another thing we've got to figure on," Bertha Cool said. "That murder rap keeps Donald out of circulation, and I need him in my business. Christ, I can't afford to pay a man five dollars a day wages and a monthly guarantee in order to have him dodging cops. There's no percentage in that.—You shouldn't have brought that up, dearie. It makes me sore as hell every time I think about it."

"Your anger," Mrs. Premmer said acidly, "your foul talk, and your very evident vulgarity don't alter the situation in the slightest. Mr. Lam is a fugitive from justice. I have only to call the police to have them take the matter in hand."

"That's right, dearie," Bertha Cool said, taking her cigarette holder and a cigarette from her purse. "Where the hell do you keep your matches? I find I didn't bring mine.—Never mind. Donald, lover, she'll get me one."

Bertha Cool calmly fitted her cigarette into the holder. After a second or two, Mrs. Premmer walked over to a smoking-table, brought a box of matches over, and Bertha held up the end of the cigarette showing that she expected a light.

Mrs. Premmer struck a match and lit the cigarette. Her hand showed only a slight tremor. She seemed pleased with herself as she went back and sat down.

Bertha said, "It will simplify matters if you'll tell us just how it all started, Mrs. Premmer."

The blonde said, "I don't know what you're talking about. I will admit that I know a Mr. Gell. Apparently, this was a name taken by a Mr. Cunner for the purpose of leading a double life. I know nothing whatever about that. I only knew him slightly."

Bertha Cool yawned.

Mrs. Premmer said defiantly, "And I'm sticking by that story."

Bertha Cool looked across at me. "Do you know, Donald, I think we're wasting time trying to give this bitch a break. We could do a lot better by going ahead with the thing the way I originally outlined it to you. She's a natural for the murder of Gell.

"You know as well as I do that girl at the telephone desk will swear that the mysterious party who drove up in the automobile was in reality a woman dressed in a man's clothes. This woman knew the ropes. She knew that Gell was in apartment six hundred, went up to the apartment, opened the door and shot him without wasting any time in preliminaries or giving him any opportunity to square the deal with her.

"That's the act of a jealous woman. Now, this girl, Ruth Marr, will testify that there was something familiar about this mysterious caller. She'll think it over and testify that the voice, the carriage, the gestures were those of Mrs. Premmer. Christ, Donald, it's a natural. We don't even need to dress it up. She was jealous because Cunner was two-timing her. The telephone girl had beat her time, and she was furious.—Come on, lover, we're wasting time here. We'll go talk with that telephone girl, and then we'll call in the police."

Mrs. Premmer half screamed, "You're a liar! The idea of that little chippy beating *my* time! She's a poor country amateur, too awkward and too easy to compete with anyone—and don't try to bluff me with that murder talk. I have a perfectly good alibi for the time the murder was committed."

Bertha Cool smiled sweetly at her. "An alibi about which you'd like to tell your husband, dearie?"

Mrs. Premmer caught her breath.

Bertha Cool took a deep drag at her cigarette, and said, "I thought so. What time's your husband due home, dearie?"

I could see that the question hit Mrs. Premmer squarely amidships.

Bertha Cool went on, "It might be advisable to have our little conversation concluded before he comes in.—Don't you think so?"

"He's out at lodge. He may come in at any time," Mrs. Premmer said breathlessly.

"I see," Bertha Cool observed calmly. "When he comes in, do you want to explain me to him, or would you prefer that *I* make the explanation?"

"What do you want?" Mrs. Premmer asked.

"I want to know what happened. I want to know all that happened," Bertha Cool said. "After you've told me, I'll tell you how much to write down."

Mrs. Premmer hesitated. Bertha Cool went on casually, "Your husband knows me and knows what I'm working on. I made the mistake of accusing *him* of peddling the examination questions.—You see, Donald had found out that the people who called said they came from Premmer. We naturally supposed that it was Mr. Premmer. It didn't occur to us that it would be Mrs. Premmer until we found out you were Gell's mistress."

Mrs. Premmer glanced hastily at her wristwatch and reached a sudden determination. "I'll tell you everything," she said, "if you promise to protect me."

"Nuts," Bertha Cool said. "You're not in a position to ask for any promises, and I don't intend to make any."

"Then I won't talk."

"Suit yourself, dearie," Bertha Cool said. "We'll wait for Mr. Premmer to come in, won't we, Donald?—It shouldn't be long now."

Mrs. Premmer said desperately, "My God, have you no mercy, no respect for my husband's political position, for his career? Don't you care anything for our domestic happiness?"

Bertha Cool smiled affably. "Not a damn bit, dearie," she said.

"What do you intend to do with—with what I might tell you?"

Bertha Cool's smile was positively benevolent. "Cut myself a piece of cake," she said.

Mrs. Premmer averted her eyes, stared hard at the floor. After a moment, she said, "Have you any objection to my putting through a telephone call?"

"Not in the least," Bertha said casually. "It takes up time, that's all. If *you* want to have it over with before your husband comes, you'd better get started. You're not going to spar for time now and then hurry me later. I'm very slow and deliberate when it comes to getting facts, particularly facts I want in writing and—"

"Oh, all right," Mrs. Premmer said desperately. "My God, you know it all already, and I suppose that little tart at the telephone desk wouldn't want anything better than to get me involved in a scandal or even mixed up in a murder."

"You're probably right at that," Bertha Cool said conversationally. "You shouldn't let yourself come in competition with her type."

"I wasn't competing with her in the least," Mrs. Premmer declared.

"Horsefeathers," Bertha Cool observed, exhaling a cloud of cigarette smoke as she spoke.

Mrs. Premmer glanced helplessly about her. Tears welled into her eyes.

"If you're going to take time out to cry, dearie," Bertha Cool advised, "there's no use in hurrying at all. Your husband will be home, and we'll make a family party of it."

Mrs. Premmer snapped back the tears with indignant eyelashes. "All right, you hellion," she said, "I'll give it to you fast. I got to playing the races. Then I got in debt. It was made easy for me to borrow money. I didn't realized how easy at the time or why it was being made easy. Then Ralph Cerfitone started tightening the screws. He wanted me to get information on the Civil Service examinations. He wanted to know what forms of questions were to be used each day when examinations were given. He wanted to know the answers. He wanted information he could sell.

"Cerfitone was working through Cunner. I knew Cunner under the name of Gell. He was the one who loaned me the money. He held up my notes, and—well, by the time I found out where I stood, I was mixed in so deeply I couldn't stand—publicity."

"Meaning you'd been chasing around with Gell," Bertha Cool said.

Mrs. Premmer started to deny it, then changed her mind. "Oh, all right," she said. "What difference does it make?"

"What introduced discord into the family?" Bertha Cool asked.

Mrs. Premmer said, "Cerfitone found out that Gell was two-timing him. Gell had another apartment and was selling information on the side without splitting with Cerfitone. I don't know how big a graft it was. Cerfitone himself didn't find it out until yesterday."

"And then he killed Gell?" Bertha Cool asked.

"No, he didn't kill him. He was with me at the time."

Bertha Cool waved a jeweled hand casually toward the writing desk. "Write it out," she said, "and sign it."

"I'm not going to write it out. That puts me entirely in your power. It's asking too much."

"All right," Bertha said, "have it your way."

She made no move to go, but sat placidly smoking.

"You'd hold that over my head as a club as long as I lived," Mrs. Premmer went on desperately.

Bertha Cool said, "Of course I will, dearie. What the hell did you think I wanted it for?"

Mrs. Premmer came to her feet, rigid with indignation. "Damn you," she said bitterly. "I hate you. I could—I could stick a knife into your heart. I could put a bullet into that foul mouth of yours."

"I suppose you could, dearie," Bertha Cool observed calmly, "but in the meantime hadn't you better write that little note? You can make it brief if you want to, but be accurate and concise. Make it very clear. Your husband may come any minute."

Mrs. Premmer brushed back tears. She walked over to the writing desk, grabbed up a pen, and started writing savagely. Her face was a white mask of hatred.

Bertha Cool sat calmly comfortable, inhaling deep drags of cigarette smoke, exhaling slowly through nostrils which distended with appreciation of the tobacco.

I lost interest in the situation enough to doze off, feeling a warm haze surrounding me. Through the haze, I was dimly conscious of the room, of Bertha Cool's huge figure sitting in the massive chair, of the sound of Mrs. Premmer's pen moving rapidly over the paper.

I wakened slightly to attention as Mrs. Premmer crossed over to Bertha Cool and handed her the sheet of paper.

Bertha Cool read it through, then said, "Be a little more specific about your intimacy with Arthur Gell, dearie, and then sign it and date it."

"I won't put *that* on paper," Mrs. Premmer said. "I'll die first."

"Suit yourself, dearie."

Mrs. Premmer glared at her for several seconds, then strode back to the table and wrote some more on the sheet of paper. She signed it and handed it to Bertha Cool. Bertha Cool read it, blew on it gently to dry the ink, and said, "That's very nice. I think we can do business with that."

"Please go," Mrs. Premmer said. "Harry will be here at any moment."

Bertha Cool slowly ground out the stub of her cigarette in the ashtray. "How do you feel, Donald?" she asked. "Like going places?"

I shook off the lethargy which had gripped me and got up from the chair. "I'm feeling better," I said.

Bertha Cool said to Mrs. Premmer, "When we've gone, you can ring up Cerfitone if you want to."

"I don't want to. He'd kill me."

"Have it your own way, dearie, and remember you can trust Bertha's discretion as long as Bertha can trust you. Good night."

Bertha Cool beamed at me, tucked her hand in the crook of my arm, and let me lead her out through the door into the corridor. The minute we had left, the door banged shut with a slam that threatened to jar the plaster loose. Bertha Cool didn't even look back. We went down in the elevator. As we left the lobby, a short, broad-shouldered individual with a gray mustache, a florid face, and a military bearing was strutting into the place with great dignity.

Bertha Cool indicated him with a casual jerk of the head. "That's Premmer," she said.

"Now what?" I asked.

Bertha Cool beamed at me. "Well," she said, "here we are, all dressed up and no place to go. I think, Donald, it might be a swell notion for us to have some eats. I think food would do you some good."

"I could use about three cups of coffee," I said.

Bertha Cool summoned a taxicab, and gave the address of the most expensive nightclub in the city.

Chapter XII.

She ordered my dinner with the solicitous care of a mother guarding the health of her favorite offspring. She insisted that I have some hot soup, lots of coffee, a thick tenderloin steak smothered with onions.

The early editions of the morning papers were out, and Bertha, in between bites of double tenderloin steak with lots of French fried potatoes, cream gravy, and an avocado salad, digested the information contained in the news.

"What is it?" I asked, too utterly weary to care very much one way or another.

"They've worked up a fine case against you, Donald," she said. "It's a humdinger."

"What do they say?"

"They've found a police officer who identifies you absolutely as being the man to whom Ruth Marr handed a gun."

I suddenly lost interest in my food.

"Now, don't be sissy like that, Donald. You know it's just a part of the frame-up. This officer is one of the men whom you saw calling on Gell. In case the police had got you before the mobsters did, they wanted to spike your guns. So it was only natural that this officer should be a witness against you. Then any accusation you could make against him would seem like an attempt to get even."

"What does he say?" I asked.

"It seems that a friend had told him to call on Gell. He's a little bit indefinite about that. His story is that Gell had worked out a system for handicapping horses. Anyway, he drove out to see Gell the night of the murder."

"What," I asked, "makes you so certain he's one of the officers I had spotted?"

She gave me a pitying glance and said, "God, Donald, but you're green to be a detective.—You can't think anyone who wasn't already mixed in it up to his neck would come out in the open and make any statement like that, do you?"

"Exactly what does he say?" I asked.

"Well, let's see," she said, propping the paper against a water glass while she sawed off a piece of steak and shoved it into her mouth. "Let's see m'm'm'm. His name is m'm'm'm'm Louis Skadler. He works daytimes—drives a prowl car—heard that Gell was quite an amateur handicapper and liked to be friendly with the officers, was willing to give the boys a tip from time to time. A couple of friends in the department had told him to look Gell up, said Gell had an apartment at the Mountain Crest Apartments at Yucca City. He drove out there, parked his car, and was on the point of going in when he saw a woman—a very attractive young woman—come out of the alley back of the building and run frantically down the street. He thought perhaps he could pick her up and give her a lift. Then he thought she might be running away from something. He started the motor of his car and was about to put in the clutch when he saw her jump into a car that was parked across the street from the apartment house.—Oh yes, he took down the license number of the automobile, just on general principles.—You guessed it, lover. It was the agency car. He said there was some necking in the automobile. The man tried to get the girl out of the automobile. She made him drag her out. The way the officer describes it, she came out legs first and seemed to be enjoying it. Looking back on it, he feels quite certain that when he first saw her, she was carrying something metallic in her hand. He thought at the time it was a handbag, but he remembers now that when she got out of the car and walked back to the alley, she didn't have anything in her hand."

Bertha raised her eyes from the paper and grinned at me. "Pretty good story, isn't it, Donald? It works out nicely. He was a cop. If he'd been certain she had a gun, it would have been up to him to have investigated, but you see he wasn't certain—just something metallic. And here's your friend, Epsworth, coming in with some more stuff. He has reason to believe that Ruth Marr didn't go near the restroom. He remembers that you were hanging around in the lobby quite a bit of the time, and thinks that you went up in the elevator once."

Bertha pushed the paper aside to laugh heartily although silently. "What a sweet time they'll have doing a set of back flip-flops when they get word from Ralph Cerfitone to lay off. I wonder what they'll do about the killing—guess they'll pay more attention to that visitor.—Oh yes, Donald, your friend, Epsworth, says that the man wore an overcoat with the collar buttoned up around his chin and a hat pulled low, but that his voice sounded like yours and that he was about your build. Epsworth seems rather anxious to pin this on you, don't you think so, lover?"

I said, "Wait a minute, Bertha. There's something about that figure I intended to tell you."

"What figure do you mean, lover?"

"That person who called."

"Why call him a figure?"

"Because," I said, "I think it *was* a woman."

She stared steadily at me. "You mean that blonde, Donald?"

"Probably," I said.

"Why didn't you tell me before, Donald?"

"I thought you knew, the way you were talking. I should have told you. I just couldn't get going right. My mind hasn't been hitting more than two cylinders all night."

"Tell me more about it, Donald. How do you know?"

"Well," I said, "it's partially what I saw, but mostly what Ruth Marr, the girl at the telephone desk, saw. You know how it is with a woman. She'll notice things about a person's clothes that—"

"I know," Bertha Cool said. "Skip it, Donald. Give me the lowdown."

I said, "There was something funny about the bottoms of the pants legs. They were too long and had been turned up on the insides—the way a salesman will demonstrate a ready-made suit to a customer at the first try-on. Now a man would naturally have pants to fit him. Anyone who went to that apartment hotel in a borrowed pair of pants would be pretty apt to be a woman."

Bertha Cool thought that over while she broke off a piece of bread, sopped up the meat juice in her plate, then nodded thoughtfully. After a while, she said, "This Ruth Marr may be important to us, Donald. We don't want her running around loose.—Where is she?"

I shook my head. "That's more than I can tell you."

Bertha Cool watched me shrewdly. "Finish your steak, lover."

"I can't. I've lost my appetite."

"You shouldn't let little things interfere with your eating. Well, I'll go powder my nose. When that waiter comes along, tell him I want some mince pie a la mode, a big pot of coffee, and some cream, and tell him I don't want that watery table cream. I want real whipping cream."

Bertha Cool scraped back her chair and piloted her big bulk calmly and serenely toward the ladies' restroom.

I buttonholed the waiter and gave him her order, then I made a dive for the telephone booth and called the apartment hotel. "Let me speak with Mademoiselle Yvonne Delmaire," I told the night operator.

He cleared his throat. "It's rather late. She—"

"She's up," I said, "waiting for the call. This is Carl Benn of 207 talking."

"Oh," he said. "Just a moment, Mr. Benn, and I'll connect you."

Ruth Marr's voice was tearful as she said, "Hello," without accent. I figured the night clerk would be listening in. I said quickly, "Mademoiselle, I dislike to bother you at this hour, but I knew you were sitting up waiting for the call. I have covered all of the various agencies which might have anything in which you'd be interested, and I am able to report satisfactory progress."

She took a tumble and said, "Oh, I am, what you call, overjoy. It is excellentment! Perhaps I see you soon, no, yes?"

"I'll be in in about half an hour," I said, "but I'll go right to bed. I'll see you in the morning."

"Oh no, no, M'sieur. But please. You do not understand Mademoiselle Yvonne. She wait so anxiously to know the details."

"The details can wait until morning."

"Oh, but no! I am not that type, M'sieur. I cannot sleep until I know. It is not late for Mademoiselle Yvonne. Many times she reads all the night and goes to bed only with what you call the chickens." She giggled at that, and then as I kept silent, said, "Please. Promise me, M'sieur, for a moment, for five minutes, perhaps, when you come, you will look in on me just to tell me the details."

I figured the more she talked, the more her idea of a foreign accent was going to get full of hayseeds. The night clerk was probably a dumb egg, but even so he might have ideas. Hell, he might even have taken one of those correspondence courses and been able to talk to the waiter in French.

"Okay, Mademoiselle," I said, "but it may be late," and hung up the telephone before she had a chance to do anything else with her Midwestern ideas of the accent on an Albanian refugee who had been educated in a Paris convent.

Bertha Cool was back at the table by the time I left the telephone booth. If she'd been powdering her nose, she certainly hadn't done any loafing. I circled around so that I approached the table from the general direction of the men's room. Apparently she didn't see the detour, nor did she look up at me until I drew back my chair. She was smoking, and her eyes, blending into the pale color of the cigarette smoke, studied me thoughtfully through the haze. "Hurt much, lover?" she asked.

"Rather sore," I said, "but getting better."

"How does the food make you feel?"

"Okay."

"Think you're good for any more shocks tonight?"

"No," I said. "Whatever it is, it can wait until after I've had some sleep."

She said, "I guess it can at that," and then, after a moment, "I wish I'd known about that damn blonde when I was talking to her. I'm afraid I let her off too easy."

"She isn't off yet," I said.

Bertha Cool smiled, a slow, ominous smile. "You're damn right, she isn't, lover.—I don't think you'd better go back to your room."

"I won't," I said.

"Your clothes are up in my apartment. You'd better stay there tonight, Donald."

"No, I don't think that would be wise."

She thought things over for several puffs at the cigarette. The waiter appeared with her mince pie a la mode, the coffee, and a pitcher of thick, yellow cream. Bertha creamed the coffee, watched the globules of butterfat rise to the surface and melt, and nodded approvingly as she dumped in three heaping spoonfuls of sugar. "Well, Donald," she said, stirring the coffee slowly, "I guess perhaps you're right. I have an old suitcase up there. You can put your clothes in that and wear the evening clothes until you get settled.—It's a good to remember about cops, Donald. They never say anything to a man in evening clothes if he's sober.—A tuxedo, yes, but full dress, no. Of course, if you get drunk, it doesn't work, but all you need to do is put on tails, and you can walk right out of a jewelry store at three o'clock in the morning with a satchel under your arm, say to the officer on the beat, 'Good morning, my man. Will you please check this door to make certain it's locked,' and he'll touch his cap to you and call a cab for you."

I wasn't particularly interested in her dissertation on police psychology. I looked down at the demitasse and wondered if I wanted any more coffee. I was beginning to feel wide awake.

"When you get this thing cleaned up," Bertha Cool went on, "you'll have to get out of the country."

"Out of the country? I asked, startled.

She nodded.

"Why," I asked, "if we have it cleaned up?"

She said, "You went to Judge Longan, lover."

"Well, what about it?"

"He'll expect to hear from you."

"Well, is there any reason why I can't tell him about Cerfitone?"

Her look was pitying. "Is there any reason," she said. "Listen, lover, Bertha tried to cut herself a piece of cake. The knife slipped. Bertha almost cut her fingers. So then Bertha had to go get flour, eggs, butter, cream, and mix up her own cake. Now she's getting ready to put it in the oven. And you want to come along and tell Carter Longan the whole recipe so he can publish it in the newspaper."

I said, "I can't leave the country. He'd figure I was covering up."

"He wouldn't figure anything of the sort," she said. "As a matter of fact, you won't even know you're leaving the country. Bertha will simply give you a job shadowing someone. It will be someone who's taking a boat for Honolulu, Australia, and Singapore. You'll tail along as a part of your regular job. It'll be a nice vacation for you, Donald. You'll have the ocean trip and all your expenses paid. You'll draw wages while you're gone.— You know, Bertha, lover. She wouldn't cut herself a piece of cake without getting some for you."

I said, "I virtually promised Longan I'd let him know if I found out anything about Cerfitone."

"A virtual promise is nothing," she said. "Don't be a sap, Donald. You can't get anywhere tying up with a reformer— because a reformer can't get anywhere. People are suckers, Donald. God made them suckers. Politicians lead them around by a ring through the nose. Occasionally, some reformer comes along and beats the cymbals and blows the trumpet—and that's all the good it does."

"No, it isn't," I said. "The people sweep the corrupt officials out of office."

Bertha beamed at me. "Sure they do, lover, and then what happens?—They elect a reformer."

"Well, what of it?"

"And then what happens to the reformer, lover? He either has to build up a political machine or else he's defeated at the next election. If he builds up a political machine, he has to do it by distributing gravy to the boys who are on the inside.—Hell, Donald, politicians *always* have cake. The people pass it to them on silver platters, and when the politicians cut it, they have to cut a piece for each of their friends. Otherwise, the friend becomes an enemy.—My God, Donald, don't make the mistake of trying to protect the dear people. You can't protect a man from himself. You don't suppose you could talk to a sheep and turn him into a bull, do you?"

I said hotly, "That's not the same thing. Essentially, people are honest. They—"

"Sure, they're honest," Bertha Cool interrupted, "but they're lazy, and they're mentally inefficient. They like to be hypnotized. They love to be fooled, and they're suckers for sales psychology. Look what happens, lover. We have graft today. A hundred years ago we had graft. We probably have more today than we had a hundred years ago. For three generations now people have been following reformers, fighting all sort of graft.—And what has it brought them, sweetheart? Not a damn thing, except more graft than when they started. No, Donald, precious, people are sheep. They were made to be sheared. They love to worship public officials who play politics. Every eight years, the people swallow some politician hook, line, and sinker and make him president. They hold him on the political stomach for about six years. Then they commence to get indigestion because the politicians quit pouring the soda bicarbonate of publicity into their stomachs. At the end of eight years, they vomit him up in order to swallow someone else, and the process is repeated.

"Why, listen, lover—of course, you aren't very old, but did you ever hear of a politician who wasn't elected on a platform of economy in office?"

"That isn't it," I said.

"Oh yes it is, lover. I can remember way back. Even then all politicians were promising economy, and still it wasn't new. They'd always hold up the extravagances of the past administration before the horrified eyes of the voters. They'd pledge greater economy and get elected.—And there's never a case on record, lover, where a politician hasn't spent more than his predecessor in office."

"Oh nuts," I told her. "What's the use?"

She smiled at me. "That's the spirit, Donald. You'll just have a job tailing someone to Australia. That's all you'll need to know about it, lover. When you get that job, you'll know that Bertha Cool has cut herself a piece of cake, and has wrapped a nice little piece up in waxed paper for Donald.—But you're tired, lover. You mustn't sit here and argue. Meet me tomorrow at ten-thirty for breakfast in the tea room of that department store where we had lunch last week. They'd never think of looking for you there. Let me have another cup of coffee, and we'll go home. You need some sleep. You're too puny to take two beatings in one night."

"You be careful," I warned. "They'll know about Mrs. Premmer's confession by now. They'll kill you to get that."

Bertha Cool's diaphragm rippled in a chuckle. "I'll take a hell of a lot of killing, lover."

Chapter XIII.

Ruth Marr answered my gentle knock on the door of her apartment. "Well, for the love of Mike, look at *you*!" she exclaimed, her eyes sweeping up and down my full dress.

"Well, for the love of Mike, look at *you*," I countered, taking in the silk dressing gown with the rose-colored mules peeping out from underneath the trousers of pajamas which seemed to be composed of black silk netting.

She modestly drew the robe more tightly about her.

I came in and closed the door. "Look here, baby," I said, "I gave you that hundred and fifty bucks for emergency money, not to go buy a trousseau."

"I had to have something," she said, "a toothbrush and— You wouldn't want me to go around in the altogether, would you?"

I passed up that lead, walked over and sat down.

"Don't you like it?" she asked, turning slowly around so I could see the robe, and then, at the last, with a quick burst of daring, pulled the robe open so that I could see the full expanse of the black openwork pajamas with the white outlines of her form showing as a pearly-tinted background.

I felt something in the general vicinity of my heart execute antics inside my sore chest, but I remembered how deeply despondent she'd been over feeling that her love life had got out of control and burnt out the brakes. So I merely said casually, "Uh huh."

"I don't believe you like it at all," she said, pouting.

"I'm tired," I told her. "I'm too weary to appreciate beauty.

I couldn't even be bothered to look at the fan dancer at the nightclub."

"Well," she asked naively, "what did that fan dancer have that I haven't got?"

"A fan," I said, fishing a cigarette out of my pocket.

"Oh, Donald, don't be like that, so hard and cynical and unappreciative. It's not like you."

She came toward me then, her hands stretched out to me, her gown trailing in the breeze behind her.

"Back," I said, holding up my hand in a gesture of an intersection cop halting traffic. "I'm sore."

"Donald, you're not sore at me?" she cried, dropping to her knees and putting her arms around me.

I yelped with pain and said, "Christ, no, I mean I'm *really* sore. I've been beaten up. I think a couple of my ribs are smashed."

"Oh, you poor, dear boy! Let me see."

Her gentle fingers crept past the barrier of white starch that Angus had given Bertha Cool for the occasion. "Poor boy," she said sympathetically. "Tell me about it, honey."

I gently disengaged her hand and said, "Now listen, baby, this afternoon you were bawling all over my coat because your self-control had gone out of adjustment. Don't start teasing the animals."

"Donald, don't be like the other men," she said. "I didn't mean anything. I was just trying to help you—just as a nurse would do."

"A nurse," I said, "would be wearing a starched uniform, and she'd have a fever thermometer ready to jab into a patient's mouth at the first sign of acute convalescence."

Ruth Marr swung around to a sitting position on the floor at my feet. She clasped her hands over my knee and looked up at me. She said, "Gosh, Donald, you have—well, guts."

"I feel as though I had guts right now," I said. "Tell me about what happened here."

"Nothing," she said. "The clerk called a couple of times to ask if I wanted anything. He explained it was because I didn't speak good English. He thought perhaps I might be wanting to do some shopping or something or perhaps to make a telephone call."

I frowned. "I don't like that," I said.

She disengaged one forefinger to trace the outline of my kneecap through the Scotchman's rented trousers. "I fixed it all up," she said.

"What did you tell him?"

"Oh, I gargled a lot of accent at him and told him that Monsieur Benn was attending to everything."

"You went out to get those pajamas?"

"Yes."

"Where did you go?"

"Two or three places. I couldn't get just what I wanted in the smaller stores."

"Is that what you call keeping out of circulation?"

"I didn't go anywhere I didn't have to go to get what I wanted."

"Did you think they'd let you wear an outfit like that in jail?"

"No, but I thought that—well, Mademoiselle Yvonne would wear things like this, wouldn't she?"

There was an answer to that one, but I was too tired to think of it. The chair felt comfortable. The exploring progress of the tinted fingernail around the knee of the trousers was vaguely disquieting, but the warmth of her body against my leg was comforting. She said, "Why all the glad rags?"

"It was an idea Bertha Cool had," I said.

"Did it work?"

"Uh huh.—Her ideas usually do."

"Where is she now, Donald?"

"Home."

"What did you do? Have you made any progress?"

"Uh huh."

"Donald, don't be like that. Tell me about it. This means a lot to both of us."

"Uh huh."

"Well, what did you do?"

"Found the blonde," I said.

"Donald, tell me, was it Mrs. Premmer?"

"Uh huh."

"Well, what happened? What did you do?"

"Bertha Cool did it—Mrs. Premmer kicked through with a statement."

"A complete statement?"

"Uh huh."

"Did she say anything about—about you know what?"

When I didn't answer that, Ruth Marr looked up at me and said, "Donald, I do believe you're going to sleep sitting right there in that chair. Tell me, honey, was she—had she—you know. Were they—"

I tried to think of the answer with my eyes closed, but there didn't seem to be any hurry about it. I didn't know whether I should tell her the truth or whether I should stall along. She had long ceased to care anything for Cunner in the sense that she had any affection for him, but it had hurt her pride to think that the blonde had walked off with him. She—Yes, I suppose— After all, it might be better—

Her voice woke me up. "Donald, you're asleep."

I struggled my eyes into wakefulness, said thickly, "God, Ruth, I've had a night!"

Her hands moved above my knee as she hitched herself closer to me, looked at me, and said seductively, "I *could* wake you up, you know."

"Nix on that blonde line," I said. "You're better when you're just yourself—"

And that's the last I remember.

Cold, hard daylight was filtering through the drapes when I opened my eyes with a start. I was lying on the floor. There was a pillow under my head, a blanket thrown over me. The floor was carpeted, but hard and uncomfortable all the same. I moved, and it felt as though every joint in my body was being pulled apart. I groaned and settled back into my original position. I turned my head. There was another pillow on the floor beside me. It bore the imprint of a head. I felt of the carpet. It was still warm. I touched the pillow. It was wet where she'd been crying.

I heard her in the bathroom splashing around, and then, after a while, she came out, wearing the same robe without the pajamas. Where it flared out in front, I caught a glimpse of peach-colored underwear. She said, "Oh, Donald, you're awake. I didn't know what to do. I felt so sorry for you, but you were all in, and I didn't dare to try to get your clothes off. I only got off the tie and collar. That was the least I could do."

She flung aside the drapes, and morning sunlight poured in to make the room seem close and stuffy. She raised the window, looked out at the sky, and said, "It's going to be a wonderful, sunny day. What do we do for breakfast?"

"Hanged if I know," I said thickly. "I guess we eat it."

"Why, Donald, you have the most original ideas."

I grinned and found I could twist my lips without making my face sore.

"How does the chassis feel by this time?" she asked.

"I think the rear axle is out of joint," I said. "The door won't latch, the upholstery is shot to hell, and it's full of body squeaks."

"How about a nice hot tub?"

I thought that over. The idea seemed good—all except getting to the bathtub.

She went into the bathroom. I heard her singing a lilting little song, then heard the sound of water running into the bathtub. After four or five minutes, she came back and said, "All ready. What do we do next?"

"Well," I said, "I guess I try getting up."

She stood over me and gave me a hand. I worked up to a sitting position. I felt as though I was coming apart, but found that I was still in one piece. I finally managed to get up and look down at the wrinkled remnants of what had been a very doggy suit of full dress.

Ruth Marr looked at me and burst into laughter. "For heaven's sakes, Donald, get those clothes off! You don't know how woe-begone you look; evening clothes without a collar, a stiff, starched shirt that's a ruin, and clothes that have been slept in."

"Where," I asked, "do I undress?"

She indicated the room with a gesture. "Spread 'em out any place," she said. "I'm going out in the kitchenette and get some breakfast. I laid in some supplies. How would you like a big tomato juice with a lot of Worcestershire sauce?"

"And some lemon," I said.

"And lemon," she added.

"Swell," I told her.

She breezed out into the kitchenette. I draped clothes all around the place and managed to get through the bathroom door without scraping off any paint. I splashed cold water on my face, cleaned my teeth with a bath towel wrapped around my forefinger, and finally climbed into the luxury of a warm bath. I lay there letting the hot water do its stuff, feeling like a tea leaf, hard, dry, and brittle, but gradually expanding back into limp shape as the hot water soaked in.

Ruth Marr casually opened the door of the bathroom,

walked in quite calmly, and stood over the bathtub, handing me a big glass of ice-cold tomato juice with Worcestershire sauce and lemon squeezed in it. She seemed as utterly casual about it as though I'd been sitting in a chair at a lunch counter.

I gulped down the tomato juice, and handed her the glass. Without a word, she walked out of the bathroom, gently closing the door behind her.

Some ten minutes later, I walked out in my underwear, and found the suitcase which Bertha Cool had loaned me. I opened it, and it was empty.

"Hey," I yelled, "where are my clothes?"

She came out of the kitchen, calmly and competently went to the door of the closet, and brought out my suit, neatly pressed and on a hanger.

I looked at it. "For the love of Mike, when did this happen?"

"What?"

"The valet service."

"Oh," she said, "while you were asleep, I pressed it out a bit with an electric iron and a damp cloth. There's an iron furnished with the apartment, and the suit looked awful, Donald."

"Didn't you," I asked, "get any sleep?"

"A little," she said.

"Where?"

She shifted her eyes for a moment, then brought them back to mine. "On the floor beside you."

"That," I said, "was a hell of a place."

"I couldn't lift you into to the bed, Donald, and you were sleeping so soundly.—Well, I thought it would be better to leave you that way."

"I have an apartment of my own downstairs," I pointed out.

"I know, but you were in no condition to be left alone.—And that's the coffee boiling over."

She whirled and ran toward the kitchen.

I dressed and went over to look at my whiskers in the mirror. They weren't so bad. There was probably a drugstore on the corner where I could pick up a safety razor, or I might have time for a barber.

Shortly after that, Ruth called, "Breakfast's ready, Don."

I went into the kitchenette and sat down at the breakfast nook. She sat across from me pouring the coffee, urging me to try the scrambled eggs and bacon, as solicitous as a bride, as matter-of-fact as though our relationship was of long standing.

I felt better. The food tasted good. I ate, and she sat across from me, her eyes following every move I made. They were big, solicitous eyes, watching me with tender concern. I don't think she ate over two or three bites herself.

After a while, when I had finished eating and was lighting my cigarette, she said, "What did Bertha Cool do to the blonde, Don?"

"Plenty," I said.

"Did you tell her about the pants on the man who did the killing?"

"I told her about the pants," I said. "They weren't on the man who did the killing."

"What do you mean?"

I looked across at her, and said, "You know what I mean, Ruth. You killed him."

Her eyes remained calm, steady, and tender. "Donald, darling," she asked, "do you really believe I killed him?"

"You killed him," I said. "Anyone but a sap would have known it when you came out carrying the gun. Like the boob that I was, so far as women are concerned, I fell for it."

She put her elbows on the table, interlocked her fingers, and placed her chin on them. The robe parted enough to show me the peach-colored slip, her firm white breasts and the long sweep of her throat. "How long," she asked, "has it been since you—felt that I killed him, Don?"

"Ever since I talked with Bertha Cool last night, and she read me the statement the officer had made, the one who saw you coming out of the alley back of the apartment house.—Did you know he saw you, Ruth?"

"I knew some man drove up in a car. I looked at him just long enough to see that it wasn't you. I was looking for the car you'd been driving the night before. I ran down the sidewalk. I heard him start the motor again. I knew he was going to pick me up—try to, I mean. You know how it is with things like that. A woman can tell when a man is going on the make for her."

"Can she?" I asked.

"Of course."

I said, "I could go for another cup of coffee, Ruth."

She got up and poured the coffee. "More cream?" she asked.

"Please."

She creamed the coffee, and reached over my shoulder to drop in two lumps of sugar, then she went back to the other side of the little table in the breakfast nook and sat perfectly still watching me smoke and drink the coffee. After a while, she said, "What did you tell Bertha Cool?"

"I threw Bertha Cool off the track," I said.

"How?"

"I told her just enough to start her thinking, but not enough to let her thoughts get any place. I fixed it so she thinks the blonde dressed in her husband's clothes and went up and killed him."

"Why did you do that, Donald?"

"To protect you."

"Do you want to protect me, Donald—feeling that I've killed a man?"

"Evidently, I do," I said, and then, after a moment, put down the cigarette and went on irritably, "I don't know how the hell I feel. When you told me all this line of hay about being raised in the country and thinking you were a nymphomaniac, I fell for it. When you told me Gell was the fourth man you'd been intimate with, I fell for *that*. I sympathized with you. I listened to what you said and knew that I was a damn fool for believing, but I believed just the same. I made up my mind that I'd never make a pass at you, that I'd try to get you back on speaking terms with your self-respect, that I'd try to see you got the necessary psychological attitude to enable you to throw your hooks into the next man who appealed to you, and lead him to the altar."

"That was the way you felt last night?"

"Yes."

"How do you feel now?"

I looked up at her and said, "For God's sake, cover up your breasts and quit looking at me with that worshipful look in your eyes. Jesus, I know it's phony, but it does things to me just the same."

She waited a moment, and then drew the robe in around her so that it covered her breasts.

"What are you going to do this morning, Don—just wait for developments?"

"Hell, no," I said, surprised at the rasping note that had crept into my voice. "You can't wait for developments in this business. You have to do something.—And damned if I know what to do. I can't pin the kill on that blonde, no matter what a little bitch she's been. I don't want to see you dragged into it, although what I'm doing right now is compounding a felony, making myself an accessory after the fact, and a few other things. I'm damned if I know what I *am* going to do."

I scraped back my chair, started for the door, then turned

and said, "One thing I'm going to do is get shaved. Another thing is go see how far Bertha Cool has worked on the bum steer I gave her last night."

She got up and came to the door with me, her arm resting gently on mine. "So you know that I was lying to you yesterday?" she asked.

"Hell, yes," I said.

"That I killed him and that I'm—bad?"

"It depends on what you call being bad," I said. "I know that you killed him, and I know that you've been making goo-goo eyes at me and that you planned things so I'd go on the make for you last night. I suppose you figured that you had to throw yourself in as part of the bargain, that I couldn't be trusted to protect you unless you gave me that, too."

I put my hand on the doorknob and twisted it savagely.

"When will I see you again?"

"I don't know."

"Do you want me to wait here?"

"Yes. And if you answer the telephone, remember to turn loose your accent."

She tilted her face up to mine. "Goodbye, Donald—darling."

Her lips were close to mine, her eyes seeming to swim into my consciousness. I let go of the doorknob, and grabbed her. She pushed her lithe body to mine. Her mouth seemed to melt around my tongue.

Twenty, thirty, forty seconds, or maybe a minute later, I pushed her away and dashed out into the corridor, angrily jerking the door shut behind me.

I was just a damn sucker, falling for a woman with the most beautiful body I'd ever seen, lying to Bertha Cool who was employing me, flirting with a murder rap which was going to get me sure as hell, and being too much of a sucker to even cash in on the benefits I was entitled to as fall guy.

In the elevator, I began to take mental inventory. What would happen when the murder rap caught up with us? Would she stand by me—or would she duck out from under and leave me holding the sack—the guy who killed Eben Cunner?

I didn't know the answer, but I knew the answer that Bertha Cool would give if she knew what I knew.

My job was to keep Bertha from finding out.

The clerk who had been on duty when I came in about three o'clock in the morning was still at the desk. "Good morning, Mr. Benn," he said, deferentially.

"Good morning."

His smile was smirking. "Did you get the note I left under your door this morning?"

I thought that one over, and then met his eyes with a cold, hard stare. "What was in it?" I asked.

"Just a receipt for the week's rent you'd paid on the apartment."

I held his eyes. "After this," I said, "don't ever put anything under my door."

"Yes, Mr. Benn."

I stared at him until the sophisticated smirk left his lips, but I could feel his eyes following my back out through the door.

Nuts to him.—Did I get the note under my door?—A neat little trap he'd laid, and I'd walked into it. How much did he know? How much did he suspect? He had a job that enabled him to read the newspapers from front to back, plenty of opportunity to think over what he'd read. Was he going to connect Mademoiselle Yvonne Delmaire, with her synthetic accent, and Carl Benn, who didn't get the notes which were put under his door, with the Ruth Marr and Donald Lam for whom the police were so diligently searching?

There was an answer to that—and it was something else I didn't have the nerve to put into words.

Chapter XIV.

Bertha Cool was right as rain about one thing. No one would ever look for a male fugitive from justice in the tea room of a department store. Aside from clerks and floorwalkers, I don't think there were over half a dozen men in the entire store, and those were dejected-looking individuals being dragged around by determined women.

Despite having stopped at a barber shop, I got to the tea room first, sat down, and ordered a pot of coffee. I'd bought a late-morning newspaper, and was just opening it when I looked up and saw Bertha Cool moving along with that flowing walk of hers which, coupled with her massive size, created such an impression of power.

"Hello, lover," she said.

I went through the motions of getting up to hold a chair for her, and she was woman enough to like the masculine attention. I saw her beam at me in high good humor as I sat down across from her. "You're a nice boy, Donald," she said, "a nice, well-mannered boy—and you lied to me, you bastard."

"What now?" I said.

"That report about tailing Cunner from the Orange Cove Apartments up to the Mountain Crest Apartments."

"Haven't you got over that yet?" I asked.

"No, lover. I'll always be sore about that. It's an unpardonable sin in this business—tell me just how you happened to lose him, lover."

I said, "When that last car drove up, I dashed down the street to get a hamburger. When I came back, the car was gone and so was Cunner. I didn't know what to do. I stalled around for a while, and then beat it out to the Mountain Crest Apartments, and there he was."

Bertha Cool ordered a big pot of coffee, a pitcher of whipping cream, fruit juice, cereal, scrambled eggs, little pig sausage, a side order of hot cakes, and lots of maple syrup. I told the girl to bring me dry toast and coffee.

"What's the matter, lover? Don't you feel well?"

"I can't get up much appetite for breakfast."

Bertha Cool made clucking noises of sympathy. "You can't fight the world, Donald, unless you keep up your vitality, and you can't keep up your vitality unless you train your stomach to take on nourishment whenever it can get it.—Well, Donald, let's go back to that place where you faked your report. I think it's important."

"Why is it important?" I asked. "He was at one place, and he went to the other. The time element is such that there wasn't any chance for him to do any loitering along the way."

"I know, Donald, but just the same it's important."

"Why?" I asked.

"I don't know," she admitted, "except that it's always the case. The part of a report a detective fakes is always the part that holds the key clue. Now get to work, Donald, and figure it out for us."

And Bertha Cool poured half a pint of whipping cream on her cereal, snowed it under with gobs of sugar, and gave herself up to the wholehearted appreciation of eating.

I nibbled at my dry toast, and said, "Well, a speed cop called on him. His business took fifteen or twenty minutes. Then, after a while, a couple of dicks in a prowl car came up, and I figured it would take them at least as long, maybe twice as long. So I beat it down the street in search of a hamburger place."

"I know, lover. You told me that before."

"When I came back, they were gone."

Bertha Cool nodded and went on with her eating.

I toyed with the toast and sat staring at the plate. Then I said, "I suppose, of course, that means something, if you want to figure it that way. The last two men didn't stay as long as they should."

"That's better, Donald. Go ahead and think from there."

I went on drawing conclusions. "The reason they didn't stay as long as the others had or as long as I supposed them to is that they didn't come for the same purpose. The others came to get tipped off to examination questions and work out a deal. These men came for some other reason. Perhaps it was to tell Cunner to beat it from the Orange Cove Apartments out to the Mountain Crest. If that's the case, he must have started almost immediately after they arrived."

Bertha looked up at me with pride in her eyes. "Donald, you're the brainiest little bastard I ever had working for me. You've hit it. That's exactly what happened. Now go ahead and tell me *why*."

I thought that over for the time it took me to sip half a cup of black coffee, and then said, "Probably this is the answer. Cunner was supposed to take that apartment at the Mountain Crest Apartment House under the name of Gell, and peddle the information the inner circle wanted him to peddle, but he saw no reason why he shouldn't have a shakedown on the side—just as Mrs. Premmer told us. So he got this apartment at the Orange Cove. He wasn't playing a lone hand. He couldn't. He needed some point of contact. That point of contact had to be different from the one he was using in the other apartment. That point of contact was getting a split on the Orange Cove business.

"Now then, right after the shooting, Cerfitone knew about the Orange Cove Apartments. He went there—got there almost as soon as we did. We knew about them *before* the shooting. It's reasonable to suppose that Cerfitone did too."

Bertha Cool nodded thoughtfully, dumped more sugar into her second cup of coffee.

"Well, Cunner left the Orange Cove Apartments in a hurry. That must have been because he had a tip-off that Cerfitone knew about the place. That tip-off must have come through the two officers who drove up. Therefore, those two officers must be the ones who were his point of contact in the Orange Cove branch of the business.—That would make the thing figure this way: Two or three nights out of the week, Cunner was supposed to take the name of Gell, and go to the Mountain Crest Apartments to peddle information for Cerfitone and his gang. The rest of the time he was supposed to be home with his family. Instead of that, he got an apartment at the Orange Cove Apartments, and bootlegged information on the side. Cerfitone found out about it. The two officers who were standing in with Cunner drove up and gave him the alarm. Cunner's only hope was to show that the guy in the Orange Cove Apartments was two other people. So the officers dumped him into the city car, opened the siren, and made time up to the Mountain Crest Apartments."

Bertha Cool said, "Donald, my love, I don't know why I should bother trying to think when I have such a brainy little bastard working for me."

The waitress brought the huge stack of hot cakes, scrambled eggs, little pig sausages, looked at me solicitously, and said, "Don't you care for anything else?"

I shook my head.

"Is the toast all right?"

"Fine," I said.

Bertha Cool said to the waitress, "Don't expect me to eat this stack of hot cakes with only four squares of butter. Go get me some butter, dearie, and when I say butter, I mean butter."

The waitress flashed a bright smile and went away.

"Now then," I said, "if Cunner wanted to get to the Mountain Crest Apartments in order to convince Cerfitone that he hadn't been at the Orange Cove Apartments, he'd naturally have wanted Cerfitone to know that he was at the Mountain Crest Apartments. That means he'd have telephoned him as soon as he got there.—But I don't think he did that because Ruth Marr would have told me if he had."

Bertha Cool said, "He was smart, Donald. He stopped at a public telephone as soon as he got away from the Orange Cove Apartments, called Cerfitone, and told him he was at the Mountain Crest Apartments, and if there were any more customers to send them out. He figured that he'd get to the Mountain Crest Apartments before any customers arrived or before Cerfitone telephoned."

Bertha heaved a deep sigh. "Well, lover," she said, "that gives us the picture. Cunner thought he was fooling Cerfitone, but he wasn't smart enough. Cerfitone probably didn't bump him off, but he could have arranged things very nicely. I'd pick Alfred as the trigger man. Cunner thought he was pulling the wool over Cerfitone's eyes. All he was doing was telling Cerfitone where he could be found so he could keep an appointment with the undertaker."

I thought that over, breaking up the toast into small pieces.

Bertha Cool paused in the process of shoveling in grub to say, "One other thing, Donald."

"What?" I asked.

"I've been checking up on that officer who said he saw the girl run out of the alley with the gun and jump into the agency car.—I don't think he's one of the gang. The records show that he wasn't taking any Civil Service examination."

"So what?" I asked.

"So, lover, that would make him right," she said, "and the girl did come out of the alley and did give you the gun."

I didn't say anything.

Bertha Cool went on, "That's the worst of you, Donald. You'll never make a success in this game until you lick that weakness of yours. You have lots of brains. You can figure things out when it's just a problem that Bertha puts up to you across the breakfast table. But when it comes to actually meeting people, you lose your perspective. You're too impressionable, Donald. You pick some little tart and fall in love with her every time."

"Ruth Marr isn't a tart," I said indignantly.

"Now don't get your bowels in an uproar, Donald, because Bertha is just telling you for your own good."

"All right," I said hotly, "I'm telling you for your own good. Ruth Marr isn't a tart. Lay off her."

Bertha Cool went on calmly, "You've figured it out yourself, Donald, even if you did try to send me on a blind trail. Cerfitone is the one who had Cunner bumped off, but the girl was the one who did the actual killing. Therefore, she's working for Cerfitone. She might have got jealous and—no, that doesn't account for it.—It must be this way, Donald. She's Cerfitone's woman. Cerfitone got her the job in the Mountain Crest Apartments so she could spy on Cunner and keep him honest. He probably told her to make a play for Cunner, and then by manipulating things so Mrs. Premmer and Ruth Marr got at sword's points, Cerfitone was in a position to play both ends against the middle. The worst of getting a woman spy to be a man's mistress is that sometimes they really fall for him. By using two of them, he figured he could lick that angle. When he found out he was being double-crossed, he told Ruth Marr to turn the heat on Cunner."

"I don't believe it," I said. "It's not true."

"Yes, Donald, darling you *do* believe it. I can tell from the indignant way you say that it's not true, that you're really trying to convince yourself. It all reasons out, lover. Two and two make four."

"Well," I said, "Cerfitone can't get away with it."

"Why not?"

I leaned forward and said, "I'll tell you why. He's carrying a thirty-eight caliber Smith & Wesson revolver in a shoulder holster.—The gun that he's carrying isn't the gun that he *thinks* he's carrying."

"What gun is it, lover?"

"The gun that killed Cunner," I said.

Bertha Cool slowly deposited her knife on one side of the plate, her fork on the other. She looked at me for several seconds, then an angelic smile broke out on her face. "Donald," she said admiringly, "you little son of a bitch.—I told Cerfitone that you were plain poison, and the damn fool wouldn't believe me. So the girl really *did* give you the hot gun. I knew she had, of course.—Well, Donald, you're clever. You're damn clever. Now, what are you going to do?"

I said, "Let's follow this thing to its logical conclusion. Cerfitone found out that Cunner had this double-cross apartment. Before he could do anything about it, two men showed up and whisked Cunner away. We've just demonstrated that those two men must have known all about the double-cross apartment and the gravy that Cunner was getting on the side. Here's something we haven't considered. Those two men must also have been sufficiently close to Cerfitone to know *exactly* when Cerfitone found out about the apartment in the Orange Cove. Therefore, these two men must be playing both ends against the middle too. They must have been close to Cerfitone—

so close that they knew the minute he found out about Cunner's double-cross—and then they helped Cunner put the double-cross over."

Bertha said, "That's swell, lover. Go right ahead thinking out loud. Don't let it bother you if it doesn't interfere with my eating—because nothing interferes with Bertha's eating, lover."

I said, "I'm going to let Cerfitone know that these two men double-crossed him."

"What good'll that do?"

"It'll probably start some shooting," I said, "and if Cerfitone shoots, he shoots with a hot gun. The police will check on the bullets."

"And accuse Cerfitone of Cunner's murder?" she asked.

I nodded.

Bertha Cool put more maple syrup on the hot cakes. "And I don't suppose you care whether Cerfitone actually killed him or not?"

"Why should I care?" I said. "Cerfitone is a crook. No matter who killed Cunner, Cerfitone ordered it done. He was the real one who was back of it."

"It's all right, lover," she said, "except you're overlooking one thing."

"What's that?" I asked.

"Cerfitone had him killed all right, but it was this girl of yours who did the killing. When Cerfitone gets in a hot spot, he'll squeal. When he squeals, he drags Ruth Marr into it. She drags you in."

I said, "Ruth Marr didn't do it."

She laughed, and said, "You try to say that convincingly, lover, but you can't even convince yourself. You *know* she did it.—This business of the woman with the pants doubled up is something she thought up to alibi herself."

"I saw that woman get out of the car," I said.

Bertha Cool smiled indulgently and shook her head. "You're such a nice boy, Donald. It's a shame you have a weakness of falling for women the way you do."

The waitress approached somewhat diffidently and said, "Are you Mrs. Cool?"

Bertha shoveled in the last of her hot cakes and said, "Yes. What is it, dearie?"

"You're wanted on the telephone."

Bertha said reassuringly to me, "Elsie Brand is the only one who knows where I am. I told her if she had to telephone to go out and use a public pay station somewhere. I'll be back in just a minute, Donald."

She followed the waitress toward a telephone booth.

I sat there and thought things over.

The waitress came back and hovered solicitously over me, pouring hot coffee into my cup. "This will warm it up for you," she said with a smile. "—Don't you want anything else?"

"No," I said, and then, to reassure her, added, "I've already had breakfast."

"Oh," she said with a smile, "I was getting worried about you."

She kept hanging around until Bertha Cool came back. Bertha gave her a shrewd glance, and, when she had left, said, "There's another one, Donald. That waitress is all wrapped up in you. I don't know what it is you do to women—or what women do to you.—Well, lover, you won't tell Cerfitone anything."

"Why?" I asked.

"He was picked up out near Yucca City. He was lying in the ditch off to one side of a road near the Mountain Crest Apartments. He's suffering from a severe concussion and probably a skull fracture. They've taken him to the emergency hospital."

I caught the eye of the waitress and motioned. She stopped in the midst of taking an order at the other end of the dining room and came hurrying solicitously toward me.

"Could I have a telephone put here on this table?" I asked.

"Certainly," she said. "I'll get it right away," and kept the others waiting while she brought me a phone and plugged it in.

Bertha Cool watched me with curious eyes but said nothing.

I called the number of Judge Longan's office. I told his secretary to tell the judge that I had to speak to him personally upon a matter of importance, that I was the same young man who called on him yesterday with reference to irregularities in the Civil Service Department.

Bertha Cool ordered another pot of coffee, another pitcher of whipping cream, and told the waitress to fill up the sugar bowl.

After a few moments, I heard Judge Longan's voice on the telephone. He was cautious but eager.

I said, "You know who this is talking, Judge?"

"My secretary told me what you said to her," he observed noncommittally.

"All right," I told him, "you know who it is then. Have you heard the news about Cerfitone?"

"What news?"

"He was found unconscious out near the Mountain Crest Apartments," I said, "and was taken to an emergency hospital."

"Well?" he asked.

"Cerfitone carries a gun," I said.

"With a permit which was issued him by the police department," Judge Longan said acidly.

"While he's unconscious," I said, "you might have the ballistic department fire a test bullet from that gun and compare it with the bullet which killed Cunner."

His voice showed excitement. "Look here, is this on the level? Where are you now? I want to talk with you. I—"

"It's on the level," I interrupted, "and you've already talked with me." I dropped the receiver back into place. When the waitress returned with Bertha Cool's coffee, I said, "That's all. You can take the phone away now."

Bertha Cool said, "Cerfitone wouldn't listen to me when I told him what a little rattlesnake you were. You *are* a mean bastard, Donald."

I said, "I believe in justice."

Bertha Cool stirred whipping cream into the coffee and said, "How about a cigarette, lover?"

I shook my head.

She opened her bag, took out a cigarette, lit it, and sat in tranquil contemplation, letting her breakfast digest, blowing out placid clouds of cigarette smoke. After a while, she said, "I found out something else too, Donald.—Elsie just told me."

"What?" I asked.

"This Mrs. Atterby is very wealthy. She own quite a bit of property."

"She's a battle-ax," I said.

Bertha nodded, her eyes fixed dreamily on the spiraling smoke from the cigarette. "You know it would be nice," she said, "if Bertha could cut herself two pieces of cake."

"Wouldn't it?" I said sarcastically. "I might get a raise in my monthly guarantee—not a lot, but enough to live on."

Bertha said, "Don't be like that, lover," without even turning her eyes toward me. After a while, she went on, "Do some more thinking, Donald. I like to watch your mind work."

"I've been doing it," I said.

Bertha shifted her eyes from the cigarette smoke to stare at me. "You believe in playing them close to your chest, don't you, lover?"

Something in her tone caught my attention. "What else," I asked, "did Elsie Brand report?"

"Just routine, darling.—If Ruth Marr gets involved in this, she's going to drag you in, Donald—not that you aren't dragged in already."

"Ruth didn't kill him."

She laughed and said, "That's why you're so eager to make a fall guy out of Cerfitone I suppose?"

"Shut up," I said savagely.

"All right, lover. Have it your own way. Why don't you try cream and sugar in your coffee? It would build you up."

"I don't want it."

"Well, don't bite my head off, Donald."

We sat there in silence for a few minutes. The waitress said to me, "Could I bring you some more hot coffee?"

"Just a check," I said.

Bertha Cool said reassuringly to me, "Listen, Donald, if Bertha Cool could cut herself two big pieces of cake, she'd see that you had your share. Bertha isn't ungrateful."

I didn't say anything.

The waitress brought the check. I passed it across to Bertha. She paid it and left a ten-cent tip. I picked up the ten cents, put it in my pocket, took a half dollar from my pocket and put it under my plate.

Bertha watched me with tolerant eyes. "You mustn't be like that, Donald," she said. "You're too soft when it comes to dealing with women."

I said, "How would you like to go out and call on our client?"

"I wouldn't like it, lover."

"I think you should."

"They're nursing their grief, Donald."

"But I think it would be a nice thing to express our condolences."

"They know you're wanted by the police."

"We could," I said, "extend them sympathy in their hour of bereavement."

She looked at me sharply then, and said, "Donald, have you been doing some more thinking?"

I didn't say anything.

She ground out her cigarette and pushed back her chair. "Why the hell didn't you say so?" she asked.

Chapter XV.

Mrs. Atterby answered the bell after we had rung for the second time.

She was clad in black. Her eyes, deep-set, and shaded beneath somber brows, seemed to reflect the mourning of her costume.

She spoke to us in a whisper as though words would profane the situation. "The poor, dear child is taking it *terribly* hard. I never realized how much she loved him."

Bertha Cool said, "When's the funeral?" much as though she'd been saying casually, "When do we eat?"

"We don't know," Mrs. Atterby said, in a voice which fairly oozed the hush of death. "The authorities say we can't make our plans until after the inquest. I think they're holding the inquest tonight—the poor, dear child."

"Where is she?" Bertha Cool said. "We want to see her."

"Oh, but you can't see her."

"Let's go in, sit down and talk things over," Bertha said.

"I'm sorry. I can't invite you in. She mustn't be disturbed—"

"Oh nuts," Bertha Cool said and walked on past her through a reception corridor and into the living room. I tagged along behind. Mrs. Atterby, her mouth set like the edge of a razor blade, followed us. "I must say, Mrs. Cool," she said, "that I consider your intrusion very ill-timed. Your work has been of no possible advantage to my daughter. I presume it's useless to ask you to refund any of the money which we paid. I blame myself in part for bringing Edith to you. The poor, dear child will always have that as a horrible memory now, and your reports were—hardly tactful."

"Bring her in," Bertha Cool said. "Let's see her."

"But, my dear Mrs. Cool, *can't* you understand? Edith is very sensitive, very high-strung, very nervous. She has been through a most horrible ordeal which has left her entirely unstrung. I presume a woman in your profession and of your temperament can never appreciate what—"

Bertha Cool, fitting a cigarette into her long, ivory cigarette holder, looked across at me and said, "Give us a match, Donald."

I lit her cigarette.

Mrs. Atterby held up her hands in horror. "Please, Mrs. Cool," she said. "I'm trying to be polite about it. Edith cannot and will not see you. She—"

At that moment, the door opened and Edith Cunner came waking into the room, her eyes swollen and pink-rimmed, her manner that of a martyr staggering toward her doom. She said plaintively, "I couldn't help hearing what you said, Mother, dear. It's Mrs. Cool, isn't it? What does she want?"

Mrs. Atterby ran to gather Edith to her bosom. "My poor, dear child," she said. "Mother wanted to spare you from as much of the ordeal as possible. I presume these—persons—want to—"

"We don't want to take up a lot of time, Mrs. Atterby, and certainly don't want to intrude upon Mrs. Cunner's grief. We just want to take a look at the closet where Mr. Cunner kept his clothes."

Mrs. Atterby snapped her eyes around to me as a scientist might look at a fishworm. "What is it you want?" she asked.

"To look at Mr. Cunner's clothes."

"His clothes?"

"Yes."

"What possible bearing can his clothes have upon your employment? We hired you for a specific purpose. There is no longer any necessity for that employment. I'm going to have to ask you to leave."

"I'll leave," I said, "as soon as I've seen Mr. Cunner's clothes, but I have to see them."

"Why?"

"You may know that I'm mixed up in this thing," I said.

"I read in the papers that your presence was deemed highly suspicious. I—"

"All right, I want to see his clothes," I interrupted.

Mrs. Atterby looked at her daughter. "Edith, dear," she said, "could you be brave and stand the ordeal? I think it's perhaps the best way to get the interview over."

Edith choked back sobs and bravely nodded her head. Bertha Cool said in an undertone of disgust, "Oh Christ."

I got to my feet. Bertha Cool also arose. Edith Cunner led the way toward a bedroom door. Mrs. Atterby hesitated a moment, then started to follow. I brought up the rear with Bertha Cool.

Bertha turned to me and said in an undertone, "You brainy little bastard! Why didn't you tell me, lover?"

I didn't say anything.

Mrs. Cunner entered a bedroom, a room on the ground floor with twin beds. On the pillow of one of the beds was a floral wreath. Mrs. Atterby turned to us and said, in an aside, "The poor child takes his loss so seriously. I didn't realize she loved him so much."

Mrs. Cunner opened the closet door.

I looked in at an assortment of masculine clothes, hanging in a neat array.

"Just what is it you want?" Mrs. Atterby asked.

Edith Cunner's sobs became more audible, reaching the crescendo of hysteria.

I looked through the clothes and didn't find what I wanted.

"Is that all?" Mrs. Atterby asked acidly.

I went through the suits in a second search. "Are these all?" I asked.

"We don't know what he has elsewhere," Mrs. Atterby said pointedly.

"My darling, dead Eben!" Edith Cunner wailed.

"You poor child," Mrs. Atterby said, and then to Bertha Cool, "You see what you've caused. Her nerves are worn to a ragged edge."

I stood there in the closet door, thinking.

Mrs. Atterby said, "I think you'd better go now."

There was a bathroom door at one end of the room, another door at the other. I nodded toward it. "Where does that go?"

"That's Edith's closet," Mrs. Atterby said. "And I'm going to ask you to leave us alone now."

I walked across the room and jerked open the closet door. Dresses, feminine shoes, and a shelf of feminine hats greeted my eyes.

Mrs. Atterby said, "I must insist that you tell us the reason for these strange actions, Mrs. Cool."

Bertha Cool said, "Take your time, Donald. I'll handle this pair."

I dove into the closet. I found what I was looking for in the back and brought it out, a plaid, double-breasted suit. "What's this?" I asked.

Mrs. Atterby said, "The suit Eben wore the last time he took Edith to the theater."

"Don't touch it," Edith Cunner said. "I'm keeping it to remember him by. I want him buried in that suit."

I stripped the coat from the hanger and took out the pants. Edith Cunner threw herself at me, circled me with her arms, and screamed, "Don't touch it, I tell you."

Mrs. Atterby grabbed my collar. "Such vandalism," she said.

Bertha Cool moved with unhurried efficiency. I saw her arms swing in a swiftly powerful motion. Mrs. Atterby went stumbling across the room in one direction. Edith Cunner was jerked half around and pushed over to the bed at the other side of the room. She fell back across the floral wreath. Mrs. Atterby screamed, "Call the police, Edith."

I held up the pants for Bertha Cool's inspection.

Eben Cunner had been a long-legged man. These pants had been tucked back and folded underneath. They had been basted some six inches up the inside of each leg.

Edith Cunner, scrambling from the bed, started to run from the room. Bertha Cool reached out and grabbed her with one hand. "Well, I'll be goddamned," she said. "So you traced the registration of that car, found out he was registered in the Mountain Crest Apartments, went there, and killed him."

"You lie," Edith Cunner screamed. "You're crazy. You don't know what you're saying."

Mrs. Atterby said, "The law deals with such people as you, Mrs. Cool, and as far as this little shrimp, I think the police will be interested in knowing—"

I buttoned the top button of the trousers so that Bertha Cool could see the waist measurement. "Not Edith," I said. "She's too fat."

Bertha Cool looked at the trousers, then up at Mrs. Atterby's strained, drawn face. "For Christ's sake," she said slowly, and then after a moment, "Donald, my love, the party's going to get rough. The police still want you. Take the agency car and get the hell out of here. Meet me at the place where you met me this morning in about an hour."

I hesitated, and while I hesitated, Mrs. Atterby came for her in a rush.

I'll say one thing for Bertha Cool. She can hit like a man.

Her fist caught Mrs. Atterby flush on the jaw. She said, over her shoulder to me and without looking back, "Beat it, lover."

I beat it.

I had an hour. God knows what Bertha Cool intended to do, but I felt she was fully capable of handling the situation. I drove to the apartment hotel. I had forty-five minutes to spare on my appointment, and I wanted to see Ruth Marr.

There was a new clerk on duty at the desk, a day clerk whom I hadn't met. Evidently, however, he knew all about me. "Mr. Benn?" he asked when I came in and paused at the desk for my key.

I nodded.

"There's a note for you," he said. "Mademoiselle Delmaire asked me to see that you got it as soon as you came in."

I tore it open, and read the shaky note in Ruth Marr's handwriting.

"This is goodbye, Donald, sweetheart. I could never face you again. It is better for you, better for me that we go our separate ways. A way has opened up for me to leave this all behind and begin over again in a new environment. Don't try to find me, but remember that I love you always.

Yours, Ruth."

I looked up at him vacantly. "Where," I asked, "is Mademoiselle Delmaire?"

"She checked out," he said. "There's no forwarding address. Can I be of any assistance, Mr. Benn?"

I pushed the note in my pocket, said, "No," and walked out of the hotel.

The women who had begun to flock into the tea room sat around gabbing and eating. They stared at me as though they thought I was crazy. I couldn't stay in one place. I'd sit at the table for a while, smoke cigarettes, then get up and walk to one of the windows. Bertha Cool's hour had become an hour and a half. The waitress who had taken my breakfast order that morning was particularly solicitous. I told her that I wanted to be left alone, that a party was joining me for lunch.

It seemed ages before Bertha Cool came in, calmly competent, serenely unhurried. She walked across to the table, said, "Hello, Donald," and then to the waitress, "I want a pot of black tea and some French pastries.—What are you eating, lover?"

"Nothing," I said.

"Sit down."

I sat down. Bertha Cool carefully fitted a cigarette into the long, ivory holder. "Jesus, Donald," she said, "but I've been a busy woman."

"What," I asked, "have you been doing?"

She looked surprised that I'd asked the question. "Cutting myself two pieces of cake," she said.

"Just what does that mean?" I wanted to know.

"It means, Donald, that I have a new job for you."

"What?"

"A ship sails for Honolulu at two o'clock this afternoon. There's a party aboard who is sailing for Honolulu, Pago Pago, Suva, Australia, Samarang, and Singapore. I want this party shadowed, and Elsie Brand is arranging your transportation. She's buying clothes for you. You'll find them in your cabin in new suitcases. The tailor on the ship can make any alterations you'll need. We've telegraphed for a passport. There'll be some papers for you to sign. You can pick up your passport in Honolulu."

"Look here, Bertha," I said. "I can't do it."

"Why?"

"In the first place," I said, "you're compounding a murder."

"Nuts," she said. "You can't convict anyone of murder on a pair of pants with the legs folded back."

"And there's Judge Longan," I said.

"Don't be silly, lover. He has all the evidence he needs—more than he can use. He's going before the grand jury this afternoon.—It will be a fine vacation for you, lover. You need the sea air. The job won't be arduous. Once you're aboard the ship, your party can't give you the slip. All you have to do is take life easy, sit in a deck chair, read, relax, and get your nerves under control. Remember, lover, what Bertha Cool said. She wouldn't cut herself a piece of cake without seeing that you had a slice."

I shook my head doggedly.

"Your wages," Bertha said, "will go on from the time you leave port until you get back.—Jesus, Donald, you're a devious little bastard! You've put Bertha to a lot of trouble following your back trail and figuring out what you've done."

"Suppose I don't go," I asked.

"You'd be on a spot, Donald. They'd subpoena you before the grand jury. You'd make a lot of charges which couldn't be substantiated. You'd be under oath and have to commit perjury or else tell the true story about that gun. That wouldn't sound nice for you, Donald, and by the time you get done you'd be convicted of something or other."

"How about Mrs. Atterby?"

"There's some very weak circumstantial evidence against Mrs. Atterby," Bertha said, "nothing on which anyone could pin an actual charge. The case against Cerfitone is much stronger, but he can beat the murder rap. In order to beat it, however, he'll have to come clean on the rest of the stuff. It's going to bust the city wide open."

I thought things over. "Who's paying for this?" I asked.

"I am," Bertha said, and then, with a reminiscent smile, "Don't forget, Donald, that when Bertha Cool cuts herself cake, she cuts nice, generous slices."

I did some more thinking. The waitress brought Bertha Cool the French pastries and a pot of black tea. "Isn't there something for you, sir?" she asked, looking at me with pleading eyes.

"A cup of coffee," I said.

"Right away," she told me and hustled toward the kitchen.

Bertha Cool glanced at me across the rim of her teacup.

"What time does the boat sail?" I asked.

"Two o'clock."

"How about this person I'm to shadow? Will you give me a description?"

"Yes," Bertha Cool said, "that will be arranged. It's a young woman, Donald. Her name is Mademoiselle Yvonne Delmaire. She's a fugitive from one of the Albanian states, a very attractive young woman, I understand—with a tragic past."

And Bertha Cool deftly speared a French pastry and transferred it from the platter to her plate. Her eyes were twinkling with humor. "Now try to say 'no,' you little bastard," she said.

Afterword
By Russell Atwood

FRY ME FOR AN OYTSTER:
The Apprenticeship of Donald Lam

The Knife Slipped was intended to be the follow-up to *The Bigger They Come* (1939), the first Cool and Lam mystery—until it was rejected by Morrow, Erle Stanley Gardner's publisher.

But Gardner didn't give up on the duo; he had strong affection for these two characters. Lam was based on his literary agent, Thomas Cornwall Jackson, another "brainy little runt" (he went on to marry actress Gail Patrick, who later, together with Gardner, produced the classic Perry Mason television series starring Raymond Burr, as well as a failed pilot for a Cool & Lam series, which can now be found on the Internet with an intro by the author himself). Even though Gardner is best known for creating Mason, one of fiction's greatest detectives, he said he got more pleasure writing the outrageous adventures of Bertha and Donald than he did the more serious cases of the better-known lawyer-sleuth.

Turn on the Heat (1940) eventually became the second book in the series that went on to span 29 books, the last, *All Grass Isn't Green*, published in 1970 after Gardner's death. Except now I suppose the number is 30, including this one.

It's interesting to note that the plot of *Turn on the Heat* bears no resemblance to that of *The Knife Slipped*. Gardner didn't attempt to "fix" this book, he chucked it and wrote an entirely new story. As the prolific author of over 150 books, Gardner had made himself into a veritable fiction factory, continually turning out new product. If something came off the assembly line and didn't work properly, he didn't try to repair it and send it back through again—he went back to the drawing board to design a better model that did work.

To some extent his books are formulaic, but it is not so much a formula he adheres to as a recipe he follows while adding different exotic ingredients. Gardner uniformly wrote his books around a central conflict and then spiced them with his wide range of interests and his experiences as a lawyer. Thus the reader learns how to salt a gold mine in *Gold Comes in Bricks* (1940), how to fix a slot machine in *Spill the Jackpot* (1941), and the legal difference between accidental death and death by accidental means in *Double or Quits* (1941).

What intrigued me most while reading *The Knife Slipped* was the question "what if?" What if this book had been accepted and become the second book, how would it have shaped the rest of the series differently?

There are some key differences. For one, Bertha Cool comes off as a much better detective here than she does in any of the books that follow, superior to Donald Lam in this case, which could be called one of his failures. It falls to her to be the clear-headed one and point out aspects of the case Donald has been blind to (blinded by love). If this dynamic had continued in later books, they might have developed a Nero Wolfe/Archie Goodwin relationship, with Donald doing all the legwork but Bertha ultimately untangling the mystery with her shrewd, cynical approach.

It's not that in subsequent books Gardner "dumbed down" Bertha, though in her two solo assignments that take place while Lam is serving in the Navy during WWII (*Bats Fly at Dusk* and

Cats Prowl at Night), she does need outside assistance to solve the cases. Rather it's that her interest in solving crimes is primarily "How high a fee can I charge?" If there is no payoff, why solve the crime at all? To Bertha there is a far worse crime than theft, blackmail, drug-smuggling, and murder combined, and that's expending valuable resources and not getting paid for it!

If anything, in *The Knife Slipped*, the reader encounters Bertha Cool at her most—for want of a better word—sentimental. She forgives Donald even though she knows he's lying to her face and withholding information. And then!—in the end she finances a romantic cruise for him with his lady love. This is nothing like the Bertha Cool in books such as *Top of the Heap* (1952), in which she dissolves her partnership with him, scratches his name off the door, and cancels his access to the joint bank account when he gets in serious trouble with the law (only to take it all back when he shows up with a five-figure payoff).

In the rest of the series, Donald is shown to be the real brains of the organization, but in this book he makes some rookie mistakes no self-respecting private eye ever should. He loses the man he's tailing because he goes to get something to eat. He tampers with evidence by getting rid of the gun with no real purpose in mind. His play-acting at the hotel lobby phone booths meant to divert attention only heightens the night clerk's suspicions.

His biggest error in judgment is that he believes the woman he's helping is actually guilty of the murder. He assumes Ruth's love for him is a sham, that she's only playing up to him to get his help, but he "heroically" allows her to play him for a sap. This assumption blinds him to what has really happened and prevents him from solving the murder without Bertha Cool's help.

These are mistakes of youth, and possibly Gardner envisioned a longer apprenticeship for Donald Lam in the books to come.

In a way, *The Knife Slipped* was ahead of its time, departing from the model of the infallible hard-boiled detective completely in control of the situation no matter how complicated it got. Instead Gardner wrote of a young man getting in over his head and making mistakes. It may be that the publisher rejected the book back in 1939 for just that reason: readers weren't ready for a detective flailing around, doing the wrong things for the wrong reasons.

However, whether this book wound up published or not, I believe Gardner needed to write about this early failure in Lam's career, to create a backstory to better inform the character and make him more human. The Donald Lam that emerges in *Turn on the Heat* is less of a cocky know-it-all, he has humility without falling into the cliché of self-deprecation. He's a man that appears to have paid his dues. That's why I feel this book is an important addition to the series: it serves as a "lost" episode showing how a great detective isn't born, but made.

WANT MORE
COOL & LAM?

**If you enjoyed THE KNIFE SLIPPED,
the lost Cool & Lam novel by
ERLE STANLEY GARDNER,
you'll love his classic**

TOP of
the HEAP

When a gangster's beautiful girlfriend vanishes, the last man to be seen with her goes to P.I. Donald Lam for an alibi. But the client's story doesn't add up, and soon Lam's uncovered a mining scam, an illegal casino, a double homicide, and a chance for an enterprising private eye to make a small fortune—if he can just stay alive long enough to cash in! Discover where Donald and Bertha go next in this classic Cool & Lam mystery from the creator of Perry Mason.

**Read on for an excerpt
From TOP OF THE HEAP!
Available now from your
favorite bookseller.**

Chapter I.

I was in the outer office, standing by the files, doing some research on a blackmailer, when he came in, all six feet of him.

He wore a plaid coat, carefully tailored, pleated slacks, and two-tone sport shoes. He was built like a secondhand soda straw, and I heard him say he wanted to see the senior partner. He said it with the air of a man who always demands the best, and then settles for what he can get.

The receptionist glanced at me hopefully, but I was dead pan. Bertha Cool was the "senior" partner.

"The *senior* partner?" she asked, still keeping an eye on me.

"That's right. I believe it is B. Cool," he announced, glancing toward the names painted on the frosted glass of the doorway to the reception room.

She nodded and plugged in to B. Cool's phone. "The name?" she asked.

He drew himself up importantly, whipped an alligator-skin card case from his pocket, took out a card, and presented it to her with a flourish.

She puzzled over it for a moment as though having difficulty getting it interpreted. "Mr. Billings?"

"Mr. John Carver Billings the—"

Bertha Cool answered the phone just then, and the girl said, "A Mr. Billings. A Mr. John Carver Billings to see you."

"The Second," he interposed, tapping the card. "Can't you read? The Second!"

"Oh, yes," she said, "the Second."

That evidently threw Bertha Cool for a loss. Apparently she wanted an explanation.

"The Second," the girl repeated into the phone. "It's on his card that way, and that's the way he says it. His name is John Carver Billings, and then there are two straight lines after the Billings."

The man frowned impatiently. "Send my card in," he ordered.

The receptionist automatically ran her thumbnail over the engraving on the card and said, "Yes, Mrs. Cool," into the telephone.

Then she hung up and said to Billings, "Mrs. Cool will see you now. You may go right in."

"*Mrs.* Cool?" the man said.

"Yes."

"That's B. Cool?"

"Yes. B. for Bertha."

He hesitated perceptibly, then straightened his plaid sport coat and walked in.

The receptionist waited until the door had closed, then looked up at me and said, "He wants a man."

"No," I told her, "he wants the *senior* partner."

"When he asks for you what shall I tell him?"

I said, "You underestimate Bertha. She'll find out how much dough he has, and if it's a sizable chunk she'll ask me in for a conference. If it isn't a big wad and John Carver Billings the Second intimates he thinks a woman isn't as good a detective as a man, you'll see Mr. John Carver Billings the Second thrown out of here on his ear."

She looked very demure. "You're so careful with your anatomical distinctions, Mr. Lam," she said without smiling.

I went back to my office.

In about ten minutes the phone rang.

Elsie Brand, my secretary, answered, then glanced up and said, "Mrs. Cool wants to know if you can come into her office for a conference."

"Sure," I said, and gave the receptionist a wink as I walked past and opened the door of Bertha's private office.

One look at the expression on Bertha's face and I knew everything was fine. Bertha's little, greedy eyes were glittering. Her lips were all smiles. "Donald," she said, "this is John Carver Billings."

"The Second," he amended.

"The Second," she echoed. "And this is Mr. Donald Lam, my partner."

We shook hands.

I knew from experience that it took cold, hard cash to get Bertha to assume that ingratiating manner and that cooing, kittenish voice.

"Mr. Billings," she said, "has a problem. He feels that perhaps a man should work on that problem, that it might—"

"Be more conducive of results," John Carver Billings the Second finished.

"Exactly," Bertha agreed with a cash-inspired alacrity of good humor.

"What's the problem?" I asked.

Bertha's chair squeaked as she moved her hundred and sixty-five pounds around so as to pick up the newspaper clipping on the far corner of her desk. She handed it to me without a word.

I read:

KNIGHT DAY'S COLUMN—DAY AND NIGHT

BLOND BEAUTY DISAPPEARS. FRIENDS FEAR FOUL PLAY. POLICE SKEPTICAL.

Maurine Auburn, the blond beauty who was with "Gabby" Garvanza at the time he was shot, has mysteriously disappeared. "Friends" have asked police to make an investigation. The police, however, who feel that the young woman was considerably less than co-operative during their investigation into the shooting of the mobster, are inclined to feel that Miss Auburn, who kept her own counsel so successfully a few nights ago, is about business of her own. So far as police are concerned, her failure to pick up milk bottles from the doorstep of her swank little bungalow in Laurel Canyon is a matter of official indifference. In fact, officers pointed out quite plainly that Miss Auburn resented having police "stick their noses" into her private life a few days ago, and the police intend to respect her desire for privacy whenever possible.

The story as given to police by "friends" is that three days ago Maurine Auburn, who was the life of the party at a well-known nitery, became peeved at her escort and walked out.

Nor did she walk out alone.

Her departure was prefaced by a few dances with a new acquaintance whom she had met for the first time at the nightclub. The fact that she left the place with this newfound friend, rather than with members of her own party, is a circumstance which police consider to be without especial significance. Friends of the young woman, however, regard it as a matter of the greatest importance. Detectives are frank to state they do not consider this occurrence unique in the life of the mysterious young woman who was so singularly unobservant when Gabby Garvanza was on the receiving end of two leaden slugs.

When milk bottles began to pile up on Miss Auburn's doorstep, the peeved and jilted escort, whose name is being withheld by the police, felt that something should be done. He went to the police—perhaps for the first time in his life. Prior to that time, as one of the officers expressed it, the police had gone to him.

In the meantime, Garvanza, who has so far recovered that

he has been definitely pronounced out of danger, continues to occupy a private room at a local hospital and, despite his convalescence, continues to employ three special nurses.

After coming out of an anesthetic at the hospital following the operation which resulted in removing two bullets from his body, Gabby Garvanza listened patiently to police inquiries, then, by way of helpful co-operation, said, "I reckon somebody who had it in for me must have taken a coupla shots at me."

Police consider this a masterly understatement of fact and point out that as an aid to investigative work it is somewhat less than a valuable contribution. There was a distinct feeling at headquarters that both Gabby Garvanza and Miss Auburn could have been much more helpful.

I dropped the clipping back on Bertha's desk and looked at John Carver Billings the Second.

"Honestly," he said, "I never knew who she was."

"You're the pickup?" I asked.

He nodded.

"And Maurine left the nitery with you?"

"It really wasn't a nightclub. This was late in the afternoon, a cocktail rendezvous, food and dancing."

I said to Bertha, "We *might* not want to handle this one."

Bertha's greedy eyes flashed at me. Her jeweled hand surreptitiously strayed toward the cash drawer. "Mr. Billings has paid us a retainer," she said.

"And I offer a five-hundred-dollar bonus," Billings went on.

"I was coming to that," Bertha interposed.

"A bonus for what?" I asked.

"If you can find the girls I was with afterward."

"After what?"

"After the Auburn girl left me."

"That same night?"

"Of course."

"You seem to have covered a lot of territory," I said.

"It was this way," Bertha explained. "Mr. Billings was to have been joined for cocktails by a young woman. This young woman stood him up. He had been attracted to Maurine Auburn, and, when he caught her eye, asked her to dance. One of the men who was with her told Billings to go roll his hoop. Miss Auburn told the guy *he* didn't own her, and he said he knew that; he was watching the premises for the man who did.

"It looked like the party might get rough so Billings, here, went back to his own table.

"A few minutes later Maurine Auburn came over to his table and said, 'Well, you asked for a dance, didn't you?'

"So they danced, and, as our client says, they clicked. He was nervous because her escorts looked like tough mugs. He suggested she shake them and have dinner with him. She told him about another place she liked. They went there. As far as Billings knows she's still powdering her nose."

"What did you do?" I asked Billings.

"I stuck around, feeling like a sap. Then I noticed two girls by themselves. I made a play for one of them and got the eye. We danced for a while. By that time I realized, of course, Maurine had stood me up. I wanted one of these girls to ditch the other one so we could go places. No dice. They were together and they were going to stay together. I moved over to their table, bought them a couple of drinks, danced with them, had dinner, paid the check, and took them to an auto court."

"Then what?"

"I stayed all night."

"Where?"

"In this motor court."

"With *both* of them?"

"They were in bedrooms. I was on a couch in the front room."

"Platonic?"

"We'd all had quite a bit to drink."

"Then what?"

"About ten-thirty in the morning we had tomato juice. The girls cooked up a breakfast. They weren't feeling too good and I was feeling like hell. I got away from there, went to my own motel, took a shower, and went down to a barbershop, got shaved and massaged and— Well, from there on I can account for my time."

"Every minute of it?"

"Every minute of it."

"Where was the motor court?"

"Out on Sepulveda."

Bertha said, "You see, Donald, these were a couple of San Francisco babes on an auto tour. Mr. Billings thinks they knew each other pretty well, that they may have been relatives, or may have been working together in an office somewhere. Apparently they'd planned an auto tour of the country on their vacation. They wanted to see a Hollywood night spot and see if they could get a glimpse of a movie star. When Mr. Billings offered to dance with them they were willing to play along but they were playing the cards close to their chest and wouldn't let the party split up.

"Mr. Billings offered to drive them in his car but they said they were going to drive their own car. He— Well, he didn't want to say good night too soon."

Billings looked at me and shrugged his shoulders. "One of these babes had gone for me, and I'd gone for her," he said. "I thought I might get rid of the chaperon if I tagged along. I didn't.

I'd had a little more to drink than I thought. When we got out to the motor court I proposed a nightcap and— Well, either they loaded it on me or I'd already had too much. The next thing I knew I was all alone and then it was daylight and I had a beautiful hangover."

"How were the girls the next morning?"

"Sweet and cordial."

"Affectionate?"

"Don't be silly. They weren't in the mood any more than I was. We'd all of us been seeing the town."

"And what do you want?"

"I want to find those two girls."

"Why?"

"Because," Bertha said, "he's uneasy now that it seems Maurine Auburn has disappeared."

"Why beat about the bush?" Billings said. "She's Gabby's moll. She knows who pumped the lead into him. She didn't tell the police but she knows. Suppose someone should think that she told me?"

"Any particular reason why she should tell you?" I asked.

"Or," he said hastily, "suppose something's happened to her? Suppose the milk bottles keep on piling up on her porch?"

"Did Maurine Auburn give you her name?"

"No. She just told me I could call her 'Morrie.' It was when I saw her picture in the paper that I knew what I'd been up against.

"The guys with her must have been mobsters. Think of me barging up and asking for a dance!"

"Do that sort of thing often?" I asked.

"Certainly not. I'd been drinking, and I'd been stood up."

"And then you went out and picked up these two babes?"

"That's right, only they made it remarkably easy for me.

They were on the prowl themselves—just a couple of janes on a vacation looking for a little adventure."

"What names did they give you?" I asked.

"Just their first names, Sylvia and Millie."

"Who was the one that you fell for?"

"Sylvia, the little brunette."

"What did the other one look like?"

"A redhead who had a possessive complex as far as Sylvia was concerned. She knew all the answers and didn't want me asking questions. She built a barbed wire fence around Sylvia and kept her inside of it. She may have loaded my drink with something besides liquor. I don't know. Anyway, she produced the bottle for a nightcap and I went out like a light."

"They consented to let you take them home?"

"Yes. As a matter of fact, they hadn't checked in anywhere yet. They wanted a motor court."

"You went in their car?"

"That's right."

"Did they register when you got to this motor court?"

"No. They asked me to register. That was the nicest way of asking me to pay the bill. In a motor court you pay in advance."

"Were you driving their car?"

"No. Sylvia was driving the car. I was sitting in the front seat next to Millie."

"Millie was in the middle?"

"Yes."

"And you told Sylvia where to drive?"

"Yes. She wanted to know where to get a good motor court. I told her I'd try and get one for her."

"And you picked this court out on Sepulveda?"

"We passed up a couple that had a sign 'No Vacancy' but this one had a vacancy sign."

"You went in there?"

"Yes, we drove in."

"Who went to the office?"

"I did."

"And you registered?"

"Yes."

"How did you register?"

"I can't remember the name I thought of."

"Why didn't you use your own name?"

He looked at me scornfully and said, "You're a hell of a detective. Would you have used your name under the circumstances?"

"When it came to putting down the make and license number of the automobile what did you do?"

"There," he said with a burst of feeling, "is where I made the mistake. Instead of going out and getting the license number of their automobile I just made up one out of my head."

"And the person who was running the motor court didn't go out to check it?"

"Of course not. If you look reasonably respectable they never go out to check the license number. Sometimes they just check the make of the automobile and that's all."

"What make of car was it?"

"A Ford."

"And you registered it as a Ford?"

"Yes. Why all the third degree? If you don't want the case give me back my retainer and I'll be on my way."

Bertha Cool's eyes glittered. "Don't be silly. My partner is simply trying to get the facts of the case so we can help you."

"It sounds to me as though he's cross-examining me."

"He doesn't mean anything by it," Bertha said. "Donald will locate these girls for you. He's good."

"He'd better be," Billings said sullenly.

"Is there anything else," I asked, "that you can tell us that will help?"

"Not a thing."

"The address of the motor court?"

"I gave it to Mrs. Cool."

"What was the number of your cabin at the court?"

"I can't remember the number, but it was the one on the right at the far corner. I think it was Number Five."

I said, "Okay. We'll see what we can do."

Billings said, "Remember that if you find these women there's to be a five-hundred-dollar bonus."

I said, "That bonus business doesn't conform to the rules of ethics that are laid down for the operation of a private detective agency."

"Why not?" Billings asked.

"It makes it too much like operating on a contingency fee. They don't like it."

"Who doesn't like it?"

"The people who issue the licenses."

"All right," he said to Bertha, "you find the girls and I'll donate five hundred dollars to your favorite charity."

"Are you nuts?" Bertha asked.

"What do you mean?"

"My favorite charity," Bertha told him, "is *me.*"

"Your partner says contingency fees are out."

Bertha snorted.

"Well, no one's going to tell anyone about it," Billings said, "unless *you* get loquacious."

"It's okay by me," Bertha said.

I said, "I'd prefer to have it on a basis that—"

"You haven't found the girls yet," Billings interrupted. "Now get this straight. I want an alibi for that night. The only way I can get it is to find these girls. I want affidavits. I've made my proposition. I've given you all of the information that I have. I'm not accustomed to having my word questioned."

He glared at me, arose stiffly, and walked out.

Bertha looked at me angrily. "You damn near upset the applecart."

"Provided there is any applecart."

She tapped the cash drawer. "There's three hundred dollars in there. That makes it an applecart."

I said, "Then we'd better start looking for the rotten apples."

"There aren't any."

I said, "His story stinks."

"What do you mean?"

I said, "Two girls drive down from San Francisco, they want to look over Hollywood, and see if they can find a movie star dining out somewhere."

"So what? That's exactly what two women *would* do under the circumstances."

I said, "They'd driven down from San Francisco. The first thing they'd do would be to take a bath, unpack their suitcases, hook up a portable iron, run it over their clothes, freshen up with make-up, and *then* go looking for movie stars. The idea that they'd have driven all the way down from San Francisco and—"

"You don't know that they made it all in one day."

"All right, suppose they made it in two days. The idea that they'd have driven from San Luis Obispo or Bakersfield, or any other place, parked their car, and gone directly to a nightclub without stopping to make themselves as attractive as possible, stinks."

Bertha blinked her eyes over that one. "Perhaps they did all that but lied to Billings because they didn't want him to know where they were staying."

I said, "Their suitcases must have been in the car, according to Billings's statement."

Bertha sat there in her squeaking swivel chair, her fingers drumming nervously on the top of the desk, making the light scintillate from the diamonds with which she had loaded her fingers. "For the love of Pete," she said, "get out and get on the job. What the hell do you think this partnership is, anyway? A debating society or a detective agency?"

"I was simply pointing out the obvious."

"Well, don't point it out to me," Bertha yelled. "Go find those two women. The five-hundred-bucks bonus is the obvious in this case as far as I'm concerned!"

"Did you," I asked, "get a description?"

She tore a sheet of paper from a pad on her desk and literally threw it at me. "There are all the facts," she said. "My God, why did I ever get a partner like you? Some son of a bitch with money comes in and you start antagonizing him. And a five-hundred-dollar bonus, too."

I said, "I don't suppose it ever occurred to you to ask him who John Carver Billings the First might have been?"

Bertha screamed, "What the hell do I care who he is, just so John Carver Billings the Second has money? Three hundred dollars in cold, hard cash. No check, mind you. Cash."

I moved over to the bookcase, picked out a *Who's Who* and started running through the *B's*.

Bertha narrowed blazing eyes at me for a moment, then moved to look over my shoulder. I could feel her hot, angry breath on my neck.

There was no John Carver Billings.

I reached for *Who's Who in California.* Bertha beat me to it, jerked the book out of the bookcase, and said, "Suppose *I* do the brain work for a while and you get out and case that motor court?"

"Okay," I told her, starting for the door, "only don't strain the equipment to a point of irreparable damage."

I thought for a moment she was going to throw the book.

She didn't.